CROOKED ROAD
STALKER

LINDA HUDSON HOAGLAND

Crooked Road Stalker

Linda Hudson Hoagland

DEDICATION

MIKE & SHERRY

MATT & BECKY

The loves of my life.

Crooked Road Stalker

Linda Hudson Hoagland

ACKNOWLEDGEMENTS

So All of It Was a Lie – Published as a short story in *A Collection of Winners* – expanded to novel in Crooked Road Stalker 2013 Publish America

So All of It Was a Lie – Honorable Mention/First Chapter – Alabama Writers Conclave – 2011

Don't Kill the Messenger – Published in West Virginia Writers Newsletter 2013

No Service – Second Place – Virginia Writers Club Spring Shorts 2012

Welcome to Whistler – Third Place – Westmoreland Arts & Heritage Festival 2012

Publish America (America Star) of Baltimore for originally publishing this book in 2013.

Victoria Fletcher, fellow author, for editing and formatting this book. She also developed the cover design for the book.

Crooked Road Stalker

CHAPTER 1

SO ALL OF IT WAS A LIE

"Excuse me, sir, could you take your seat, please," I said as softly as I could manage.

"So, all of it was a lie?" he shouted.

"No, not all of it," I replied through clinched teeth.

"What part was true?" he persisted.

"I'm not going to tell you that," I said deliberately.

"Why not?" he demanded.

"Well, there are some things that happened in my book that might shock you if you thought I actually did those things," I said with a forced smile.

"Yeah, there were some strange things in that book. The abortions, the sleeping around, did you do all of the drinking? Did you do any of that bad stuff?" he continued.

"Like I said, I'm not going to tell you. If you will look inside the front cover, you will see that it is labeled fiction," I explained loudly.

"But you said it's based on your life," he continued.

"It was loosely based on my life but that included friends and acquaintances that played a big part of my life. All or part of those shocking deeds could have been performed by me or any of the people I knew during that period of my life. A writer writes about what she knows so it is inevitable that part of my life infiltrates everything I write."

I wasn't going to allow him to goad me into admitting what part of my book really happened to me. I was fully aware that I was living in the Bible-belt and if I admitted to some of the happenings in my book, I would be condemned and ostracized.

I was already an outsider because I was not a native of the area so I did not want to be a condemned sinner and avoided by all Christians.

My life was one of work, home, and trying to sell the products of my imagination: my short stories and novels. I did not drink. I did not smoke. I did not have a life other than working and writing.

I didn't want a nosy writing fan to take either of those parts of my life away from me.

My first novel was about survival in the inner city of a large metropolitan area. The young lady in the novel grew from being a sheltered teenager, a country girl, to becoming the mother of two sons and living a life of walking on a tightrope the whole time she lived in the city. Sometimes she would teeter towards the wrong side of life where she would have to right herself and change her path; hopefully, teetering towards the right and good side of life.

My novel was explicit and real. That's what the Bible-belters didn't like. I didn't gloss it over and claim that a great revelation led the young lady to the goodness and light.

Survival was what led her and me out of the inner city.

Now, because of this nut, I was going to have to defend myself and the truth for the rest of my days. He appeared everywhere I was scheduled for a book signing.

"So it was all a lie," was the first utterance from his mouth each time.

"Fiction is what it is called. It doesn't mean it's a lie but it most likely is. Fiction is a creation of my brain. Sometimes it is loosely based on places I've been and people I know. Remember the important word here is fiction," I answered.

"How much of it is true?" he demanded.

"It is fiction!" I shouted as I turned from him to the rest of the small group of people. "Now, does someone else have a question or statement?" I said in a quieter voice as I tried to steer the conversation to another person in the small gathering.

This constant questioning and badgering was getting on my nerves. I wanted an answer as to why he made persistent appearances at my books signings and why the constant interrogation.

I had to admit that the questions stirred up the interests of the passersby. It did help the sales but it always made me uncomfortable.

I finished my book signing at the Stillwell County Public Library and I motioned to my interrogator so that I could talk to him privately.

"Sir, what is it that you want from me?" I asked him directly not wanting to run around that same bush that had been growing between us and jabbing me with its thorns.

"I want the truth," said the interrogator.

"Why? Why does it make a difference? You know my name, obviously, but I don't know yours. Tell me your name, please," I said in a controlled tone of voice.

"John Smith," he replied with a grin.

I looked at him like he had a third eye plastered in the middle of his forehead.

"Truth or fiction?" I asked skeptically.

"Does it make a difference?" he asked as he repeated my words back to me.

"No, I guess not. But – I still want to know why you're harassing me," I said with insistence.

"For the fun of it. And – because I want to know if you really did all that stuff in your book," he answered.

"Like I already told you, it is fiction based loosely on my life. I am a writer who writes about what she knows. Why don't you give me a break and shut the heck up?" I answered in a measured controlled tone as I tried to rein in my anger.

"Okay, if that is what you really want," he said solemnly.

"Why would I want anything else? Why would you even ask that?" I demanded.

"How have your book sales been?"

"Good," I answered without thinking. "Wait a minute! That's none of your business," I added as I felt my blood pump faster through my veins.

"Would you have sold as many if I had not agitated the crowd?"

"I don't know. Probably not," I said softly.

"I'm sorry. I didn't hear you. You need to speak a little louder."

"You heard me," I whispered harshly.

"You're serious. You don't want me to do this anymore?" he asked with disappointment clouding his face.

"No!" I screamed.

I turned and walked from the room. I had had more than enough of his interrogation.

John Smith was an attractive man, but not too attractive. Let's just say that he didn't stand out in a crowd as a Greek god might.

He was of average height and build. So, again, he was not the center of attention. The only person who seemed to notice his existence was me and that was because he spoke to me, trying to get me to answer his questions. The questions were always the same, just rephrased each time.

But – he was always there.

My next book event was at a library that was in St. Paul about two hours away from my home. I was looking forward to meeting and greeting the interesting faces of a new group of people.

CHAPTER 2

ABANDONED BABY

The morning was young, about 6:30 am, and the sun was trying to come up. A fog was working very hard at making itself known but I wasn't too worried. I was very familiar with the drive to St. Paul.

My mind wandered while I was driving as it always does.

"Whatever you do, don't…"

I heard many warnings from many different people who would begin their diatribe with that same phrase. Depending on the mood I was in, I might or might not heed the advice.

I understood why people balked at being told what to do. I did that on occasion. It was only human nature.

But – let me tell you a story about a simple act of kindness that very nearly got me killed and became fodder to feed my writing addiction.

I lived in a rural area of Stillwell County, Virginia which really was giving you a lot of room because most of the county was rural.

It was an area where you knew no strangers. The men tipped their hats to the ladies and the women waved demurely trying not to be too conspicuous. Of course, that observation didn't apply to all of the inhabitants especially those who were born a generation or two behind my sixty-four years.

I guess I wasn't as emotional or prone to the tears of love or disappointment as other ladies, but every once in a while I would come across something that really set me off on a tangent.

I was a writer, not of the world renowned variety, but I did get some recognition around the region where I lived. As a writer, I was prone to building a story from nothing.

I traveled a lot each and every weekend during the good weather months going to fairs and festivals where I could set up a table and tent (if necessary) to sell my volumes of fun and knowledge.

One dark, overcast early morning while on a two-hour drive to the small town of St. Paul, Virginia, I saw something on the side of the road that caught my attention. You knew how it was when you saw something out of the corner of your eye but you weren't quite sure of what you saw, or for that matter, if you believed what you saw.

The sight was needling at me so I did what every nosy person should do when they reach my age, I turned around and drove past the same place again.

As luck would have it, I was driving on an interstate so turning around wasn't as easy as it would have been on a city street. I continued to drive for a couple more miles before I reached an exit where I left the interstate only to cross the road and get on an entrance ramp taking me back to where I had come from just moments before. I drove about another five miles before I could perform the same function of exiting and re-entering the interstate so I could drive past the troublesome sight.

Suddenly I remembered an email I had received warning the recipients about a plot to get people, especially women, to stop on the side of the road to offer help. It had been printed in big, bold letters.

DO NOT STOP FOR ANY REASON!!! DIAL 9-1-1 AND REPORT WHAT YOU SAW, BUT DON'T EVEN SLOW DOWN.

Well, I had already not paid heed to the warning. I had turned around and slowed my driving speed so I could get a better look.

An infant car seat, covered as if to protect the baby, was positioned barely on the graveled part of the road edge, directly in front of a patch of trees not twenty feet from the traffic.

My heart wanted me to stop and grab that baby up so I could take it to a safe place for love and protection.

My mind remembered the rest of the email.

There was a gang initiation reported by legal authorities where gangs were placing a car seat by the side of the road containing a fake baby awaiting a woman, of course, to stop and check on the abandoned baby.

The email further stated: the location of this car seat was usually near a wooded area. The woman offering aide was dragged into the woods, beaten, and raped. She was usually left for dead.

Finally, my mind overrode my heart causing me to speed up a little so I could drive past the abandoned baby.

I glanced at the nearest mile maker, drove for about five more miles; then I pulled off the road, locked my car doors, grabbed my cell phone and called 9-1-1.

How do you tell the legal authorities that you saw an abandoned baby by the side of the road and that you just kept right on driving without stopping or caring?

"9-1-1, may I help you?" said the dispatcher.

"There is a baby infant seat on the side of the road at mile marker 79.4. It was covered like there was a baby inside the carrier."

"Was there a baby inside?" asked the dispatcher.

"I don't know. I didn't stop," I said in a barely audible tone.

"I will get someone to check it out. Thanks for telling us," said the kind dispatcher.

"May I call back and ask if there really was a baby in the infant carrier?" I asked shyly.

"Yes ma'am. Just ask for Nancy. I will be working until 3:00 pm," she replied.

I felt evil and bad when I completed that conversation. I felt so bad that I didn't want to identify myself to the dispatcher.

I was still on the road driving to St. Paul about a half an hour later when I tried 9-1-1 again.

"Nancy, please," I said into the phone.

"This is Nancy."

"I'm the lady who called earlier about a baby on the side of the road. Was there a baby in the infant carrier?"

"No ma'am, the infant carrier was gone. They must have gotten wind of your call."

"Maybe they did. They saw me slow down, turn around, and drive by again."

"You did the right thing, ma'am, calling and not stopping, I mean. There has been a warning issued for that type of scenario being dangerous because of gang involvement and initiation activities," said the dispatcher.

"Thanks for telling me that. I really felt so bad about leaving what I thought was a baby sitting out there on the side of the road. By the way, my name is Ellen. I'm a writer from this area and I hope to meet you someday, Nancy," I said with relief evident in my voice.

I was glad to arrive at the festival on the Clinch River after all of the excitement I traveled through to get there.

I had never been to this event before today so I was looking forward to the new faces.

As always was the case, I had to go looking for the person who assigned the booth spaces.

I spotted two writer friends, who had been positioned close to the entrance so I guessed my booth would be located in the same area. It seemed that those in

15

charge of booth spaces declared that all writers should be huddled together, like it or not.

I was right. My assigned booth space was next door to Jim Carson and Ken Hunt. As much as I liked and respected both men, I knew my book sales were going to be next to nothing.

I got mad at myself for thinking this day was going to be a waste of time because both of those men were set up next to me.

I pulled my car up and parked it in front of my assigned space so I could unload it. It was crammed to overload with a tent, two chairs, two tables, boxes of books, my writing notes, baskets of angel afghans, and many different totes with long handles that I could drape from my shoulders that were filled with tablecloths and bookmarks.

Because my hair was mostly gray, it signified that I might be a little old lady who could use some help. That was the time I was grateful for the gray hair because one or two healthy men would wander over to give me a hand.

"If you could get to the other side of this tent and pull on it, I would appreciate it," I said as I instructed my helpers.

After we got it stretched out, the next step was the hardest for me to accomplish.

"Could you push up on the corner until the canopy snaps into place?" I asked. "I'm so short I really have a hard time doing that."

Believe it or not, those strong men had a hard time pushing against the tension of the canopy stretching it into place and listening for the snap that signified success.

This was supposed to be an easy pop-up tent but a short woman like me had problems with struggling through the easy.

With the tent up, the rest of the display would be easy for me to do. I dismissed my helpers with a sincere thank you and sent them on their way to help someone else.

Linda Hudson Hoagland

I set up tables, covered them with cloths, and hung angel afghans up on the sides so people could see the different designs. It usually took me a half-hour to forty-five minutes to get myself situated; then, I was ready to sell.

I knew I was going to have a long day of watching Jim Carson corral the lookers, draw them into his web of stories, and sell them a copy of each of his books. It was my belief that he could sell snow to an Eskimo.

Ken Hunt was in the tent on the other side of me. We were hoping to attract the interest of those people who already had Jim's books.

There was one good thing about the location of my booth; I was able to see all of the activity that was happening on the Clinch River. People were kayaking and racing to win a prize.

I did manage to sell five books and that allowed me to earn back the money I had forked out for my booth space and pay for my gas to drive from Stillwell to St. Paul. Oh well, five more people knew about me and, hopefully, they would tell others about me. That alone made the day successful.

John Smith didn't make an appearance. I wasn't sure if I was happy or sad about not seeing his face and being challenged by his words.

My next scheduled book signing was to be in the Town of Stillwell at the Heritage Festival that was held every year to let the world know how proud we all were of being residents of Stillwell. I felt obligated to set up a tent and welcome friends and the not so friendly to my little space to look at my books. After all, I lived in Stillwell.

When a middle-aged woman walked up to my table and presented herself to me as Nancy, the 9-1-1 dispatcher, I couldn't have been happier to meet anyone in my entire life. Since that day we became friends, and I was thankful that she was my friend.

17

Because of the death of my husband a couple of years earlier, loneliness had overwhelmed me so I could use all of the friends I could get, if you know what I mean.

I arrived early at the Stillwell Library as was always my case when scheduled for an appearance. I hated to be late for any obligation.

I sat outside the building in my car scouring the faces of each and every person that entered the library.

No John Smith appeared before me to enter the library while I was sitting and watching. Perhaps he heeded my request that he not participate in my life as a shill to get people in the audience to buy my books.

Again, I didn't know if I was happy or sad that I didn't see his familiar face.

Of course, my book sales dropped without his input.

He was so-o-o right.

His combative questioning of the contents of my novel inspired interest from those in attendance.

Perhaps I would see John Smith at the next book event. I didn't want to admit it out loud, but I was looking forward to the next confrontation and the adrenaline rush that always occurred.

Strangely enough, I was beginning to not remember what John Smith looked like. I was guessing it was because he looked so very average.

CHAPTER 3

STILLWELL HERITAGE DAYS

Stillwell Heritage Days always appeared on the calendar during the last weekend in July.

I hauled my tent to Main Street and set it up so I could display my Appalachian Angel or Guardian Angel Afghans where they could be seen. My location of selling the afghans determined whether I would call them Appalachian Angels or Guardian Angels.

The middle of the summer was not a good time to sell afghans, but I was determined to try. I designed and created each piece of work making it a unique purchase. Each afghan I had on display was different, no two were alike, and I made sure of that.

My goal for the day was to sell as many books as possible. I wanted the hometown crowd to know who I was and what I liked to do. I spoke to many acquaintances that day and I was extremely proud of the six books I had already sold when Dan Dinsmore came up to my table and introduced himself.

The introduction wasn't necessary. I knew who he was. I didn't know why he was standing in front of me trying to be friendly.

I'm sure he didn't remember ever seeing me in his past, but I remembered him quite clearly.

He was a snob.

That was as plainly and as nicely as I could say it.

When I clerked for an auction company, Dan Dinsmore would have to register his name with me in order to obtain a bidder's card. Even though I knew who he was,

I was obligated to ask him to present a driver's license for identification purposes.

He didn't like to prove who he was. It was in his mind that everyone within the Stillwell County boundaries should know who he was without question. He always argued with me and gave me a bad time.

I didn't think I would ever forget him. Obviously, I didn't.

"I'm Dan Dinsmore," he said as he tried to get me to take notice of his presence directly in front of me.

"Yes, Dan, I know who you are," I said as I tried to push the sarcasm from my voice.

"You don't have an extra chair in your tent," he said in amazement.

"No sir, I don't need another chair. There is no one else with me today."

"I need to find a chair. I need to talk to you. I'll be right back," he said as he walked away in search of a chair he could borrow.

I never gave his statement or departure much of a thought until he returned to my tent with a chair in his hands.

He placed the chair beside mine and sat quietly while I talked to some possible customers.

When the front of the table was no longer filled with the presence of interested people he started, "I want to talk to you about writing a book about my life."

The smartass side of me wanted to be just that – a smartass.

"Why?" I asked sarcastically.

"Everyone tells me you can do it. I've checked with some people and your name keeps popping up. I'm willing to pay you well for the job," he explained.

I was at a loss for words. That was hard to do- make me totally speechless.

"I want you to think about it, Mrs. Holcombe," he continued.

"Ellen, call me Ellen, please," I said softly.

"Ellen, I really want you to write my story. I don't want you to answer me right now, if you need to think about it," he persisted.

"Dan, I need to think about it," I said apprehensively.

He rose from his chair, snatched it up, and carried it back to where it belonged.

A couple of hours later he was standing in front of me again.

"I want to buy your books," he said with a flourish of his hands.

"Which one?" I asked.

"One of each," he said loudly.

That was almost a hundred dollars.

I picked up one of each book, signed each one, and placed Watch Out for Eddy on the top.

"You need to read this one," I said. "This is how I write the truth. After you read it, give me a call if you are still interested in my writing your book."

I was so flattered but so irritated. I knew he didn't know me from the confrontations in the past.

The end of the day purchase by Dan Dinsmore upped my selling total to ten for the day. It was one of the best sales days I had had for quite a while.

I was having a bit of trouble trying to be happy. Dan Dinsmore's writing proposal had my mind in an uproar about what I was going to tell him if he was still serious about his request.

Of course, I would end up writing his book. I just couldn't pass up that opportunity.

CHAPTER 4

BLISSFUL IGNORANCE

Writing was always in the back of my mind, when I was young and attending school, but it wasn't until I was much older that I shoved it forward so I could set a goal for completion, or, at least, to make an attempt at setting my words to paper.

When I was young and in high school, I wanted to be a nurse. When I pursued the issue, checked on scholarships and the education, I was told I was too fat, my weight was too excessive and that I would never be able to do it.

I was overweight, sure, but I could do anything anybody else could do. I had no problem with it. I was a healthy female.

Upon that declaration from those who would have to admit me into the program, I decided I didn't need nursing.

I chose not to pursue any education until later in life. I waited a year to go to college where I studied business.

Strangely enough my life centered on nursing duties that I was not allowed to learn at a younger age. I had to live and learn to attain the necessary skills to keep my family alive.

My first major problem was when my fifteen-year-old son was hit by a car that caused great damage. You could see he had a broken leg because that was in a cast but once his hair grew out over the skull fracture, he looked normal. What he was, was a brain injured young teenager who wanted to die. It took five years for his scrambled brain to heal. It took five years of sacrifice from the entire family, not just me, to get him through his ordeal.

The broken leg that should have healed with no after effects, led to a bone infection that eventually required intravenous transfusions of antibiotics three times a day for a month. Needless to say, I learned to take care of that right away.

My husband had several surgeries within the same five-year period followed by open heart surgery. Twenty-six stints in his heart had been placed in his veins and arteries at various times after the open heart surgery.

Also, during that time my mother had mini strokes that led to the major stroke that killed her. She lived with us so we were totally involved in her health problems.

The only person who had remained employed during this period of one medical crisis after another was me. I had to make sure I kept my job in order to maintain the health insurance coverage.

As hard as it was to get myself up to go to work every day and leave my family at home, my struggle wasn't nearly as bad as those who were trying to survive.

The only time caregivers were needed to come into my home to offer help was when my mother was ill. Without the assistance of the health angels who were assigned the task of helping my mother into the shower, changing her bed, and generally keeping her company, I don't think I would have made it this far.

Maybe it was a good thing I did not become a nurse. I might have learned to be afraid of the various tasks I have had to perform.

Ignorance was bliss sometimes.

CHAPTER 5

THE PORTABLE WRITER

Writing for me was quite haphazard because of the many different hats that I have had to wear that tried to consume all of my time which made it very difficult for me squeeze in any words to be applied to paper.

However, I managed to apply those words to paper and I allowed them to accumulate until I really had the time to sort the pages, put them into some kind of presentable order, and send them off to someone who might consider publishing my works.

Lo and behold, some of them were printed.

I made no money, but I did receive a copy of my printed words in lieu of payment. I thought I was the richest person in the world because I was a published author.

Occasionally my riches increased in the monetary form but that was because I offered fiction and nonfiction books of my own doing to the public for consumption.

But – and this was a big but – if I hadn't stolen time to write all of those words, I wouldn't or couldn't be who I was today.

When I was just starting to put words on the page for the sake of posterity, I was in the seventh grade at Clay Junior High School in Scioto County, Ohio. Mrs. Ruby was my teacher and she was the first person of the educational world that I allowed to enter my secret life of wanting to be a writer.

I spent hours and hours writing and rewriting (by hand, of course) a hundred plus pages of a short story that I wanted her to read and tell me how much she liked it. Of course, she had no choice, she had to like it. If she didn't like it, I would have been crushed beyond repair.

"Your story is very good but you need to live a little more of your life so you can tell people about it realistically. Your story is full of imagination but some parts don't ring true because you have never felt the emotions about which you are writing," she told me as she smiled her knowing smile.

I took my story home and put it in a box. I took the box and placed it in the closet so it would never see the light of day again. I wasn't going to write any more. It was so hard to write in a house where you had no bedroom of your own. I slept in the living room on the sofa bed with my mother, while my brother and father each had their own bedrooms.

My writing didn't stay banished for very long. I pulled the box out of the closet and I continued to add to the pile.

By the time I was married, children got in the way of writing time along with the full time job I was contending with, not to mention a first husband who was very demanding.

Once in a while, I would add something to the box of writing, but not very often. Life was throwing too many obstacles in my path.

Finally, when I reached the age of forty, I decided I had better get cracking on my dream.

My eldest son had been involved in an accident where he rode his bicycle into a car and you can imagine which side of the collision won that war. He sustained a broken leg, abrasions, and a severe head injury. That story became a book. It took me about twenty years to get that piece of nonfiction down on paper in its entirety.

It wasn't until my fiftieth year appeared on the horizon that I realized that time was wasting away and I had no published writing to show for it.

I wrote at work during breaks, on my lunch hour, and other stolen times when I felt I could get away with it.

Book ideas popped into my brain and I worked and worked until I had six complete manuscripts in my possession, then I polished and rewrote and polished until I could present each and every one of them to someone for publication consideration.

At the age of sixty-four, I had fifteen books under my belt with many more in the development stage.

When my third husband was very sick, and that actually lasted about fifteen years, I wrote in his room as I watched him breathe. I wrote in my car where I slept many nights because I didn't have the money to rent a motel room so I would be close to Sonny because of his heart problems. I wrote in waiting rooms to keep my mind off of the death possibilities that he was facing each time they had to check him out for the damage that had been caused by his most recent episode.

All of this writing was done by hand, for me that was the best. Even if I had a laptop computer, I wouldn't have used it. A pad of paper and a pen was all I needed.

When I finally got around to entering everything into the computer, the fact that I already had the rough edges completed, building the rest of the book didn't take very long.

As a portable writer, I had proven to myself that I didn't require that "special" place to sit and compose my volumes. Nothing could be more portable than a pad of paper and a pen.

I proved to myself and the rest of the world that I could write anywhere just as long as I had an idea to work with and paper and pen.

Not having my own personal private place was a lame excuse for not writing. If that was the only excuse I could come up with, then I didn't want to be a writer in the first place.

So I wrote.

I wrote anywhere I could.

CHAPTER 6

DON'T KILL THE MESSENGER

Time and again I sent out my writings to anyone who would read them. I entered many contests and submitted many stories to the biggies like *McCall's* and *Family Circle.*

Then I waited.

Inside the envelope was a piece of paper that would make me react with pure joy, or, want to lash out and maybe kick the cat that was winding its body around my legs. Maybe I would make the deliverer of bad news pay for my unhappiness.

I wouldn't want to be my mailman, or mail person, if I must be politically correct. I wouldn't want to drive past my house and watch my moon pie face staring at me, freezing cold weather or horribly hot, rain or shine, through the opened front door.

I know I must look like an insane female ready to spring at some poor unsuspecting soul.

I could feel the changes that overtook me every time I spotted the flashing yellow light that the mail carrier attached to the roof of the white and red four-wheel drive vehicle. My mouth would set into an almost grimace and my eyes focused on the vehicle following its every slow movement. My body became rigid and I would dare anybody or anything to disrupt me from my vitally important task of mail carrier watching. I knew that mail carrier had something against me. Exactly what that something was I couldn't imagine, but – the mail carrier was out to get me, to make me unhappy, to bring me only bad news. I could feel the dislike for me all the way to my bones.

The anticipation of good news was what kept me going. The adrenaline flow of excitement and eagerly awaited happiness would fill me each and every day, except Sundays and holidays. That good feeling disappeared when I saw that flashing yellow light.

The brick wall of rejection, the sudden stop of the flow of adrenaline prodded me to blame someone, something, other than myself for my disappointment and subsequent depression.

It was the mail carrier's fault, no other, only him or her or whatever.

There were days, after I retrieved the mail from my letter box located across the road directly in front of my house that I wanted to chase after the mail person and inflict bodily harm upon that mail person for having the audacity to deposit a rejection letter in among my bills.

I would glare into the direction the mail carrier had driven, shake my fist, and curse the day the United States Postal Service came into existence.

Those who knew better would tell me "don't kill the messenger," but what else could I do?

The person who delivered my mail and the rejection letter was my only human connection to the source of my great disappointment.

On good days, and there have been a few, when the news was acceptable and the notice of publication was presented, I wanted to hug the mail carrier and shower that wonderful person with nothing but praising platitudes.

There haven't been many of those good days on which I would wish to say:

"God bless the United States Postal Service"

Just so those who need to know do know, I promise not to harm my mail carrier; not yet, anyway.

The fate or destiny of the writer has always been in the hands of the poor, pitiful mail carrier, at least until the age of the computer, and the creation of e-mail.

Now I can get my rejection letter e-mailed to me much faster than the sometimes inhumane long waiting period inspired by the U.S. Mail and the work involved in preparing a response.

It doesn't take a recipient of my e-mailed query very long to glance at my e-mail and recognize the fact that I'm not John Grisham or Patricia Cornwell.

"No" or "Not Interested" was a very quick and easy response when forwarded electronically. No longer were people needed to open envelopes; remove the contents; place those same contents into my self-addressed, stamped envelope with "No" or "Not Interested" checked properly; deliver that envelope addressed to me to the United States Post Office for the purpose of mailing it back to me.

I think I preferred the agony of enduring the long wait for the written rejection. It was nice to know that the rejecter had to do some work to let me know that my writing wasn't good enough in his or her subjective mind. Writers, please remember that the rejection slip could be coming from another person who may be having a bad day.

The e-mailed rejection only seemed to make me angrier. I couldn't strike out at my computer and beat it into submission. I couldn't afford to buy a new one.

Who would have figured that faster rejections would only serve to make me angry faster?

I have not figured out a way to accept rejection gracefully. I don't think any writer worth his or her salt ever does.

So, I chose to blame the mail carrier, the Internet, or the unknown for my disappointment and rejections. It couldn't possibly have been because I made a mistake. After all, I was a writer, and I was good at what I did.

CHAPTER 7

EDITORS TAKE NOTE

I passed through the anger at rejection stage and entered the stage of 'so what.' Maybe you didn't like it, but someone else would and I knew that.

I no longer paced the floor with nervous anticipation as I wore the carpet threadbare.

I no longer blamed the mail carrier employed by the United States Postal Service for misdirecting my mail or possibly even disposing of it.

I spoke to my children in kinder tones and offered motherly affection.

I vowed daily that I would not jump off the highest bridge if I didn't get the answer I wanted and needed.

I faced facts. There were hundreds, thousands, millions of writers in this world with whom I was competing.

When I was attending grade school I determined at that time that I would be a writer. I was taught to revere the book that I considered a prize possession if I were lucky enough to get one of my own.

This reverence for the book encompassed the writer of that book. I would touch the dust cover of the book bearing the picture of the author dreaming that one day my face would appear on a dust cover for others to see so they, too, could strive for the same dream.

When I started writing, my stories were based on thoughts and feelings I didn't know or understand simply because I had not endured the blessing or pains life had to offer.

I suffered.

I endured.

I loved.

I lived.

My imagination was fertile and my mind was agile, ready for any exercise of my words.

I wrote about the mysteries of life.

My goal was to write and write I did.

I would break through.

I knew I was on my way because occasionally I would get a handwritten note or personalized letter from editors telling me they were sorry but they couldn't use my submission.

The first rejection slip, a form note about the size of a sheet of memo paper, nearly broke my heart. All of those hours I had poured into arranging the words perfectly on that piece of paper were for nothing. I put my paper and pen away swearing to never touch them again.

I tried again and again. I've had several short stories published along with some short items in a national magazine, and fifteen books of fiction and nonfiction.

I was the proud owner of hundreds of rejection slips. This told you that I had not given up.

There were those who would scoff and say that rejection was rejection. Those were the glass-is-half-empty people.

I chose to believe that if I weren't getting closer to my goal, I wouldn't have earned the personalized response. I was a glass-is-half-full person and I was waiting with great anticipation to overflow the glass entirely.

I asked the editors of the world to take note.

This was my year.

At the end of 2006, after this was written, my first book was published by Publish America. Since that year, I have published fourteen more volumes for public consumption, whoever public might be.

CHAPTER 8

REALIZATION

Being a writer was not all it was cracked up to be. It was a struggle each and every day. Not so much with getting the words on paper, I could do that. The struggle came about when I wanted someone to read my words.

I hit the age of fifty and realized time was passing rapidly. One year was piling onto another and I had not accomplished my goal in life which was to get a book published.

I wanted to hold the solid feel of heft and weight of pages I had covered with my own words in black print for the world to see and consume.

Getting my thoughts down on paper was not my problem. Words were easy for me. Sometimes those very same words got me into trouble but most of the time I used those same words to talk myself back into the good graces of those who were angry with me.

I had pages and pages of written words but they were not bound into the book I had dreamed of all of my life.

Publication wasn't easy, not because I wasn't a good writer; but because I did not have the connections to become recognized and represented by a literary agent leading to the national publishers.

I tried time after time to obtain an agent. I got one who was a fraud and only wanted my money infused into his business. Believe it or not, that's not the way it is supposed to work. They, the agents, are supposed to pay me by finding a publisher who will pay me for my work, thus getting the agent paid for services performed.

Needless to say, I gave up and decided to represent myself.

I emailed my words to Publish America and they were accepted as publishable product.

I was so excited and happy to have someone accept me as a writer, an author of soon-to-be published words for public consumption.

I received my first box of books and I was well on my way to notoriety and recognition, or so I thought.

The world did not come flocking to my first book signing. I felt very fortunate that ten of my hundreds of acquaintances actually decided to show up and support me in becoming the next Patricia Cornwell.

Next – I had to learn to get myself into areas where I could promote and sell my books. In so doing, I must have stepped on someone's toes causing him or her to want to lash out at me inflicting on me great bodily harm or perhaps even death.

I never set out to cause harm to anyone.

I only wanted to sell my books.

Linda Hudson Hoagland

CHAPTER 9

IN THE BEGINNING

My thoughts went back to the beginning to my very first book:

"Ellen, your books are here. There are three big boxes of them. The UPS man just delivered them," said Sonny as he made no effort to hide his excitement.

"Oh, okay. I'll see them when I get home," I said nonchalantly.

"Aren't you excited?" he demanded.

"Sure, I just don't know where to go next, that's all," I said with apprehension.

"What are you talking about, Ellen?" Sonny asked as disappointment overshadowed his happiness for me and my first published novel.

It had been so hard getting the novel to the finished stage. It took years and years of trying to convince myself that my words were worthy of allowing others to read them.

"There is a lot of work that lies ahead of me, Sonny. There is going to be plenty of it, you know," I explained.

"It can't be that bad, can it?" he asked.

"It's not bad. I just don't know where to start. I'll talk to you later, okay? I've got to get back to work right now," I said as I placed the receiver on its base slowly while my mind raced.

I was brimming over with pride for my accomplishment, but I was scared to death to take the next step. It was not that it was dangerous, so that was not the reason for my fear and apprehension.

How do I begin? How do I get my books seen by those who might be interested enough to buy one?

I had been watching the daily newspaper, searching for information by or about other writers like me. Bits and pieces of news gave me the idea that I needed to set up some book signings.

How do I do that?

Being pushy was not a trait that I was familiar with from a personal standpoint. I preferred to fade into the woodwork and be a people watcher. Fading was not an option. Splash – I needed to make a splash. I needed to be seen and sought after. I needed to acquire a following that would look forward to each and every book release.

Wishful thinking? No – not really. I was merely dreaming of a possibility.

The last college, Southwest Virginia Community College, I attended where I received my three associate degrees was my first choice for a book signing.

"How do I get space to hold a book signing?" I asked the lady who answered the telephone.

"We will schedule it for you," said a kind voice representing the new facility at the college that held the rooms available for community use.

"How much does it cost?"

"There is no charge. Of course, you have to supply whatever you need such as your books and any refreshments that you might offer. We will supply the display tables and chairs for the visitors."

"Do you have any idea what a good date would be?"

"No ma'am, but the Christmas season is here. If you want to get in on your books being used as a gift, you might want to schedule it soon."

"That's a good idea. I will call you back tomorrow with a date. Is that okay?"

"The sooner, the better, the rooms are being booked rapidly," she answered.

What should I do? What date should I pick? What is the best time? Should I do it before the college dismisses for Christmas holidays? Week day or weekend?

I was usually not so indecisive, but I had never before scheduled a book signing. I had never been to a book signing.

My husband, Sonny, wasn't feeling well so I knew most of the running would fall on me even though he would want to help.

CHAPTER 10

IN ALL MY GLORY

I wanted everything to be perfect for my very first book signing and, of course, that included me.

My eyes usually were looking at the floor when I found myself standing in front of a mirror. I didn't want to see what the world would see. I didn't want to see the reason for the disapproval that was etched on the faces of my peers.

I was a woman who had struggled with her weight all of her life or, at least, since I could remember.

After many tears of regret and rage, I faced facts and learned to live with my appearance.

Now I looked at myself again. My eyes finally focused on the form in the mirror.

That was me – IN ALL OF MY GLORY.

The body wasn't perfect. It was the best I could do with what I've had to work with, but it was mine.

The five foot one inch, two hundred-pound reflection was who I was and most likely was what I would be when I ended my years on this Earth.

My first husband, please note I said first, told me that no one would want a fat slob with two children when I asked for a divorce. This hurt me. It didn't change the fact that I was overweight.

I didn't bother to tell him that in my fight to be accepted prior to my marriage to him, when I was sporting a wonderful size twelve, that I used to wear a size twenty.

I lost the weight and very nearly died trying to get to that size twelve. I had to eat less than one thousand calories a day to lose the weight. In doing so, my immune system failed to protect me from every germ floating in my path.

I waited eight years before I married the second time. I chose to wait. I didn't wait because no one was interested. I waited because I didn't want to face the pain of making another bad decision. The decision about getting the divorce was not the bad one.

My second marriage had problems that caused its death a mere six months later. The fact that I was overweight had nothing to do with the divorce the second time. My second husband didn't tell me that I was a fat slob or that no one would ever want me.

I married a third time. That was number three, just in case my first husband reads this. Husband number three was a good, loving husband, and I'm proud to say I finally got this marriage thing right.

Obviously my body as it was reflected in that mirror wasn't all bad. All of the pain and rejection only served as fodder feeding my fertile mind and thus supplying the thoughts and feelings that I used to fill my books with truth sounding words.

Ready or not, World, here I come IN ALL MY GLORY.

CHAPTER 11

THE FIRST BOOK SIGNING

At the local community college, Southwest Virginia Community College, I was going to debut my new novel, The Little Old Lady Next Door, and debut myself as an author which was the more sophisticated title for what I was – a writer.

My dad would have said the difference in those words were as simple as 'puttin' on airs.' He was taught not to live above his raising and he expected that I should do the same – so – writer it was.

I was excited and scared about the upcoming first book signing. Who wouldn't be excited? It was like giving birth to one of my sons except this time the pain I was feeling was only mental – not physical.

"Honey, what if no one shows up?" I asked my husband.

"Your friends wouldn't do that to you, Ellen," he said as he tried to soothe my frayed nerves.

"I hope not," I said as my voice faded to nothing.

I don't ever remember going to a book signing for anyone else so I was breaking new ground.

"Sonny, if I order cookies, can you pick them up for me?" I asked my husband who was eager to support my forays into the world of the writer.

"Sure, no problem, just let me know where and when."

"December 13th, that's the day I have chosen. It's awfully close to Christmas but it can't be helped. I know most everyone will already have purchased gifts for family and friends, but maybe they will buy one for themselves," I mumbled.

Things had not been going as I hoped. I wanted my books to arrive from the publisher before Christmas. They arrived the week of Thanksgiving but trying to schedule a first book signing party became an obstacle because I was competing with Christmas parties among other forms of celebration.

December 13th was the best I could do on short notice.

The 13th day of December, 2006, was a day that would always be etched in my brain. Not because of the "13" that was so prominently displayed; and, believe me, I was glad it wasn't on a Friday. Actually, it was a Wednesday and I'm not that superstitious, I added as I crossed my legs, my fingers, my eyes, and anything else that would chase away the evil spirits.

I borrowed a large coffee thermos from work that could hold two twelve cup pots of coffee. I had a couple more carafes that I filled with coffee and provided creamer and sugar for those who wanted to doctor the black coffee to suit their taste.

I purchased cups, napkins, paper plates, and plastic ware in matching colors so everything would look coordinated.

I mailed more than a hundred postcards to friends and acquaintances inviting all to share coffee and cookies with me to celebrate my first book.

Sonny dressed in his best pair of blue jeans and a new shirt while I wore a business suit consisting of black pants, a black jacket, and a black and white patterned print blouse so I would look professional.

The college provided two tables at the front of the room. One table I used for the coffee, bottled water, and cookies. The second table was where I had my book on display with several volumes ready for selling and signing.

I stood and waited for someone- anyone- to appear.

A man poked his head around the door facing and took in the sights as they were spread out before him.

I didn't know the man but he was vaguely familiar. I thought he must be a husband of one of the ladies I worked with every day.

"Hi, come on in," I said as I motioned for him to enter the room.

He walked in slowly and continued to absorb the scene. When he reached the front of the room, he picked up a book, turning it over so he could read the information printed on the back cover.

"How much is it?" he asked as he held up the book.

"$24.95," I responded with enthusiasm.

"Little high, isn't it?" he asked.

"It's the price the publisher put on it," I explained.

"I'll take this one," he said as he pulled his wallet from his hip pocket.

"Do you want me to sign it?"

"Sure," he answered.

"What's your first name?" I asked as I held my pen at ready.

"Just sign your name, that's all," he instructed.

"Yes sir," I said as I signed my name just below the printed version of the same.

He handed me a twenty and a five. As I searched for his nickel change, he walked out of the room.

"Who was that?" Sonny asked.

"I don't know," I said as I tried to puzzle out who it might be. I wanted to remember what he looked like so I could ask the ladies I worked with if they knew him. I was sure he had to be a husband of one of them.

Strangely enough, his image was fading from my memory. Too much worry and excitement going on around me pushed his image aside and completely out of my mind.

Vickie and her husband, Al, walked into the room.

"Please come on in, Vickie, Al, and get yourself some coffee and cookies," I said as I motioned toward the table filled with goodies.

A few minutes later, Brenda, Sarah, and Donna wandered into the room.

I sold three more books and then it was over.

I was disappointed that so few decided to support my writing endeavors but I was very grateful to those who did take the time to spend it with me and, of course, Sonny.

Some memories were sweet as sugar, some were painful and hard to think about, and some memories were bittersweet with the good thoughts tinged with regrets.

Why I was dwelling on the past was confounding me. There had to be a reason for me to replay my first book signing in my mind.

CHAPTER 12

AN AMBUSH

I drove to the Mercer Mall located between Bluefield, Virginia, and Princeton, West Virginia. I wanted to check it out so I could locate the bookstore before I had to do my book signing.

As I was browsing through the many books displayed, I could feel the stare.

Looking over his shoulder, she glanced in my general direction. She was hugging him but watching me. Her eyes never blinked as she focused in on me. The stare was so intense it made my skin crawl.

"What is your problem?" I wanted to scream at her – but I didn't.

I returned her stare and stood my ground. I wasn't going to let her intimidate me. After all, I didn't know why this was happening.

She was clinging onto the man standing next to her and whispering into his ear. The steady stare and her facial features let me know she was not saying sweet nothings to her companion.

I didn't know either of those people. Why would they be whispering about me?

I walked away from the scene I wanted to make.

I quickened my pace and returned to the bookstore I had exited a few moments earlier after seeing the staring woman. I kept my head down. I was short and people usually couldn't see me strolling through the aisles because the display shelves and cases towered above me.

At the end of each aisle I peeked around the tall structures checking out the remainder of the store as I hunted for the staring woman.

She was standing in front of the bookstore entrance with her stare trained on those leaving the bookstore.

"Get away from me?" I wanted to shout. "How long can I waste time in this bookstore? How long is she going to stand out front waiting for me to leave?"

I could feel the anger in my body overtaking the fear that had flooded through me earlier.

"You're just plain paranoid, Ellen," I told myself as I tried to rein in the anger. "No one is going to hurt you. No one has a reason to hurt you. You're just being stupid about this whole thing. She doesn't look so dangerous. The guy she was hugging earlier is gone and the staring woman is impatiently pacing back and forth in front of the bookstore exit," I continued.

Then she was gone.

"Time to go," I whispered loudly as I made my way to the front of the bookstore. I kept my head down and walked out into the mall. That was a mistake. I should have been pivoting my head back and forth scanning for an ambush.

"Ellen, wait a minute please. You are Ellen Holcombe, aren't you?"

I stopped in mid-stride to turn to the direction of the shouting voice.

"Ellen, please sign my book," shouted the woman as she rushed towards me brandishing a copy of my most recent mystery.

I smiled and the fear was replaced with the heat of embarrassment.

"Sure, I would be glad to," I said as I extended my hand to take the book from her.

I didn't think I would ever get used to being recognized by complete strangers and the thrill that coursed through my body when someone recognized me as an author.

CHAPTER 13

I'M WATCHING YOU

It was afternoon, about two o'clock, and I was sitting at a small table on the right side of the entrance to the Borders Bookstore at the Mercer Mall in Bluefield, West Virginia.

Stacks of two of my four books were spread before me on that table awaiting the fickle passerby to pick up one and, at the very least, read the blurb on the back cover.

I mailed over one hundred postcards to people who lived within driving distance of this mall. I hoped some of them would take the time out of their busy schedules to stop by and say "hi".

"Hi, Lady," said a familiar voice from the across the carpeted isle.

"Gerry, it's so nice to see you," I answered as I stood up to accept the inevitable hug. Gerry was a touchy-feely person so you knew the hug was coming.

The conversation was short.

"I've already spent my money," she said apologetically.

"That's fine, Gerry. It's just good to see you again."

I can't imagine Gerry being on a tight budget but maybe her economic circumstances have changed to such a degree that she must adhere to a strict spending limit. After all, it has been several years since we worked together at the Stillwell County Public Schools in the Central Office.

A young lady, who was disabled by a limp and also suffered from a slight speech impediment, was pushing a stroller that held a young boy about three years old. She was accompanied by a man who was also pushing a stroller containing a little girl around two years old. He didn't seem to be interested in my books.

The young lady picked up a copy of my latest mystery and read the back cover for a few seconds. She replaced the book and reached for my business card.

"How did you get your books published?" she asked.

Immediately I replied with the same spiel that I have used to answer that question many times.

"I use Publish America. I couldn't afford to self-publish by paying someone to print my first book. So – I had to look for a way to get my words onto paper without getting a five to six thousand-dollar loan or trying to borrow the money from family members."

"I have a series of children's books I would like to get published. How much do they charge?" she probed.

"Nothing up front, you pay them a percentage of the retail price of the published book and you basically buy the books for resale. I could afford to do that. How about you?" I answered and asked.

She walked away without answering.

Another familiar face came into view. Again, it was someone I had worked with but not at the school board office. Norma was a part time employee of the auction company where I also worked part time.

A short exchange of "hi" and "how are you?" was followed by her walking away without even picking up a book to get a closer look.

I was sitting and watching people. Most were walking slowly as they traipsed from one end of the mall to the other in search of bargains. Occasionally, I would see a person trudging along focused on a specific task.

A young lady about eighteen or twenty dressed in a white tee shirt adorned with what looked like a gothic, death-like figure, stopped to pick up my book.

"I've been thinking about writing a book," she said.

"Then you need to do it," I answered enthusiastically.

"I can't seem to get started," she explained.

"You need to make yourself sit down and just do it. Once you get past that first couple of pages, the words will flow more easily. It's like you are allowing yourself to begin a new life and that is being an author- a writer- who has something to tell the world," I said.

"Are your books going to be here later?" she asked.

"Yes, sure, my novels will be on the shelves," I answered.

"I'll be back on pay day to get one," she said.

"That's great," I added as she walked away.

I continued to watch the people. I smiled at anyone who looked in my direction hoping to entice someone, anyone, to buy a book.

Almost two hours had passed and no one had bought a novel. I hoped and prayed that when five o'clock arrived I had sold, at least, one book.

It amazed me about how much support I didn't get from my friends and acquaintances in my struggle to sell my books. I didn't have a large family that could take up the slack by showing up at my book events.

Me and my two sons - that was it for family.

I tried not to think bad thoughts about the recipients of those one hundred plus postcards. I knew that each and every one of them had his or her own life and visiting me at the mall didn't qualify as being number one on their "to do" list.

It was a slow day at the mall and the economic times had taken their toll on book-buying. Pleasure reading was something that could be put into a closet until the money began to flow a little more readily.

The strain on the faces of those reaching for their wallets was apparent in every store you entered.

One more hour to go and I hadn't sold a book. I expected that disappointment to occur in many of libraries I visited. But – the mall?

That final hour had passed.

Number of books sold "0".

I packed up my paraphernalia and walked to my waiting vehicle.

I saw a piece of paper tucked under the windshield wiper. An advertisement was what I thought it was. When I unfurled the paper the bold, black letters appeared:

I'M WATCHING YOU!!!!!!

"That's nice," I mumbled as I wadded the paper into the tiny ball and threw it onto the back seat of the car. I was so disappointed from the lack of sales that my mind would not accept the note as a threat.

CHAPTER 14

NO SERVICE

Not having sold one book on my previous excursion into the world of the reader, I had to fight to keep myself focused. The phrase 'what's the use?' ran through my mind, but I won the battle and was on the road again. It had to get better.

John Smith, where are you?

The road wasn't on the map, but I turned left anyway. I was lost, as usual, and I was trying my best to figure out where I was.

I had printed the directions off a map on the computer. I would have thought those people would have known what they were doing. It had to be me. I must have made a turn I wasn't supposed to make.

Everything was looking good until I drove onto a gravel road.

"This can't be right," I mumbled. "Nowhere in those directions did it mention pavement ending and with the road changing to gravel. Why don't they put up more route or county road numbers signs along the side of the road so a stranger can find her bearings?"

My frustration was turning to anger and when that change occurred, I would cry.

"Don't let me cry," I said as I felt the tears welling up behind my bulging eyelids.

My left turn was leading me further under the canopy of green forest. There were absolutely no signs of human activity anywhere I looked. No houses, no cabins, no signs of human existence whatsoever could be seen.

"Turn around, stupid," I told myself angrily.

Well, turning around was another problem. The road was narrow, barely wide enough to allow two vehicles to pass. The ditches on each side of the gravel road were broad and deep. If I managed to allow a wheel to drop into one of those ditches, I might not be able to get my car out of it without help.

I pulled my cell phone from my pocket.

'NO SERVICE' was prominently displayed across the lighted screen.

"Now what?"

I turned my wheel sharply to the left moving my car directly across the road completely blocking traffic, if there were any.

I jockeyed the car a little at a time until I was facing the opposite direction. That maneuver took about fifteen or twenty minutes and it disturbed no one except me. There was absolutely no traffic traveling on this parcel of Earth.

I retraced my path to the road from which I had initially turned left to enter this little piece of heaven. I turned right, driving back to civilization, I hoped.

When the road took me from gravel back to pavement, I felt a little relieved. Not too much relief, because I was still lost, but I didn't feel quite as lost as I had been.

I glanced at my map with the printed directions beneath it. Each left and right turn was labeled with a state route or a county road number and yet I had not seen any of those numbers within the past several miles. I had seen no road signs at all, come to think of it.

"How far back do I have to drive to retrace my path?" I asked angrily. "How did I get so messed up?"

I forced the tears of anger to dry up so I could continue to drive. To where? I didn't have a clue.

If I had not decided to set up and sell my books and angel afghans at a festival out in the middle of no man's land, I would not be having this problem.

"Alone – I'm always alone," I mumbled bitterly. "Why did you have to die, Sonny? I'm so tired of always being alone."

I continued driving, following the pavement for miles. Because of the fact that the road was paved, I knew it should lead me to people somewhere along the line.

I decided that when I finally found out where I was, I would proceed to get myself back home; no country festival today.

Mother Nature had been sitting on my bladder for several miles now. She was now kicking in her heels and causing me to squirm.

"There is no bathroom out here, God," I shouted as I tried to get my mind off of my painful bladder.

I was tempted to pull over to the side of the road and squat behind my car, but there was no shoulder on the road that would allow me to do that. The forests had transformed themselves into fields with crops of grazing cattle.

"I'm getting close to civilization," I said with apparent relief. "Thank you, Lord?" I shouted as I climbed from behind the wheel of my car.

"Restroom?" I asked the smiling man behind the counter.

"Back there," he answered as he pointed to the area to his left.

"Please don't let there be anybody in there," I prayed as I located the doorway to pain relief.

"Thank you, Lord," I said, once again, as I turned the handle and entered the small room.

With the pressure gone and hands washed, I exited the small, clean room, where I proceeded to walk to the counter. On the way, I grabbed an ice cold bottle of water from a cooler and placed in on the counter.

"Seventy-five cents," the smiling man told me.

"Can you tell me where the festival is?" I asked.

"You mean the one just down the street there?" he said with a chuckle.

I had completely missed the huge banner hanging across the roadway from light pole to light pole.

"Oh, I didn't see that," I answered with a rush of embarrassment causing my skin to redden.

"You had more urgent matters to take care of when you came in, didn't you?" he asked with another chuckle.

"Yes, I certainly did. Does this sort of thing happen often? I mean people rushing in here to use your restroom facilities?" I asked.

"Happens all the time. Restrooms are few and far between out in this neck of the woods," he said as he stood behind the counter.

I paid for my bottle of water and walked to my car.

"I'm here. I found the festival. I may as well stay," I said as I climbed back into my car.

The Craig County Young Farmers and Crafter's Fair was an attraction for farmers and would be farmers from the surrounding area. Of course, there were city dwellers but not the same kind as you would see in the larger cities. As a matter for fact, the cities in this rural area weren't cities. They were towns that had not attracted enough population to be classified a city.

Never the less, those who lived in the towns were called city dwellers because they did not have to tend to crops and livestock.

The Craig County event was staged at the county fairgrounds and the people who looked after all of us, that being the crafter's section, were kind and truly wonderful, patient souls.

The day was long but I did sell a few books, enough to pay my booth fee and gas. I wasn't going to be a big time success that way. I always considered myself a success if I sold one book, but that day I sold about six. That amounted to six more people who knew my name and face.

When I went to my car, I saw a piece of paper barely caught beneath the windshield wiper. Before I could reach for what I thought was an advertising flyer, the wind grabbed it and whirled it into the air and out of my reach.

I sighed as I thought about my next venture to parts unknown, Whitesburg, Kentucky, to be taken the next weekend.

CHAPTER 15

ALL IS GOOD

My writing life happened on the weekends with the necessity of work at the school board office controlling Monday through Friday. I liked to gloss over those necessary days of earning funds to continue my book selling.

After two and a half hours of driving, I arrived in Whitesburg, Kentucky, at the Appalshop for a gathering of regional writers.

The competition was a writer of unexplained happenings, several historical writers, a children's book writer, a thirteen-year-old young lady, and me, a writer of fiction and nonfiction.

The time was important to note. It was the day after the Seedtime Festival which was the big event of the area. Next year they were planning to include the gathering of authors during the festival with the enticement of paying each author one hundred dollars plus mileage. That sounded good to me. It was not often that I got my expenses paid to such events.

This was the first year of the gathering and I accepted the invitation without realizing that I would be paid for mileage and eight dollars for a noon meal. That little bit of money made the trip worthwhile not to mention the fact that I might be able to sell a book or two.

What made me eligible for this gathering was that I was a resident of the Appalachian Mountains and in most of my books, the mountains of southwest Virginia were the location of the events and, of course, I had to follow the Crooked Road, Virginia's Music Heritage Trail, to get many of them.

David Charles, the man in charge of wrangling the writers, had done an excellent last minute job of taking care of the wants and needs of fifteen individuals which included the grandparents of the thirteen-year-old and a wheelchair bound grandfather of another writer of the history of Appalachia as it related to her life.

I had noticed over the years that writers didn't always want to share the information they garnered about up and coming book events in which they intended to participate, so I was very fortunate to have discovered this event.

Nora Kelly Alden, the writer of many children's books, looked like the teacher that she was. She liked to lead the group and she hankered to grasp at every bit of control she could muster.

Two confederate characters of the South kept a running banter going allowing the levity to permeate the brick, wood, and steel structure. It used to be the Letcher Wholesale Grocery Company and it had been redesigned to serve as a loft for artists and writers with accommodations offered to the public on the first floor.

I sold only two books but it was still a success to my way of thinking. It was two books better than this morning plus the mileage and free lunch.

"Will you come back again next year?" asked Dave as I loaded books into my wheeled carriage (a plastic insulated drink cooler with wheels) to make my way to my car. "We will do better advertising and get you some money from a grant we have," he explained.

"Sure, why not?" I answered.

I made my way to the entrance with both arms loaded and waited for someone to see that I needed help with opening the door.

"All is good," I whispered to myself.

That's when I saw another note under my windshield wiper.

Again the words 'I'M WATCHING YOU' were emblazoned across the white paper except this time the letters were bright red.

It got my attention – finally.

I remembered seeing no one that had also been at the last festival I had attended. We were actually three hours driving time away from that festival. Who would be stupid enough to track me from one book signing to another over such a great distance?

CHAPTER 16

NO NOTE

The Border Bash in Bristol, Tennessee-Virginia, had grown by leaps and bounds. A couple of summers ago when Sonny was with me, we endured a very long evening without a sale and only bikers as browsers.

It was a bittersweet return to the festivities this year because my Sonny was no longer with me. I was trying my best to smile and not remember how so very much I missed him.

I was alone and I needed company. Normally alone was my preference. Sitting with me at a table for several hours watching me try to entice a buyer to look at what I was offering was not what most people would call fun. Sonny did it without complaint.

There was a gentle breeze blowing that felt wonderful but the feeling was laced with frustration because everything had to be anchored down. Stretching a bungee cord across the table display certainly detracted from the aesthetic beauty of the presentation.

As soon as I arrived, I started setting up my tables with stacks of books and my angel afghans.

I was almost finished with the display when the stomach pain started.

I tried to continue working through the discomfort but I had to sit down. The exertion of setting up my two tables in eighty degree temperatures always caused me to work up a good sweat. This time, the profuse perspiration forced me down onto the chair to wait out the passing of the pain.

I was panting like a dog or perhaps I should say like a woman in labor.

I knew my face had turned to a bright crimson. It always colored up with the slightest bit of physical activity. The added pain overpowered me and injected more color than usual. I could tell I wasn't looking normal by the concerned looks registered on the faces of the passersby.

I sat for five minutes, ten minutes, and my mind told me it was really bad this time. It had been months since my last attack. I sat five minutes more and the pain lessened a bit.

The cause of the pain had not been determined and probably never would be until I dragged myself into the emergency room one day while the attack was occurring.

That was a problem, getting to the emergency room while in pain because sometimes it was so severe I didn't think I could drive. Besides, by the time I arrived at the emergency room the pain would have lessened and I could get on with my day.

In other words, unless I was bleeding or near death, no one was going to do anything to find out what was causing the pain. I just had to live with it.

"God," I prayed, "please make it go away."

The pain finally subsided enough to allow me to move around. Instead of being red in the face, I knew all the color had drained from me completely. Along with the paleness I had acquired a complete and total tired feeling that barely allowed me to force one foot in front of the other to make my way to the car.

It would take me about three trips to the car to carry the table, chairs, and books to be reloaded for transport home.

Two middle-aged men came to my rescue and offered to carry the heavy items. I was so grateful for the help that all I could do was mutter "thank you" over and over again.

As I got close to the car I could see a dark, hooded figure watching me. My only thought was that it was way too hot to be wearing a hoodie.

I slowed down to get a better look and the figure moved behind some parked cars and then between two buildings where it disappeared.

I looked at the windshield.

No note was under the windshield wiper of my car.

I wished I had seen the hoodie wearer's face.

CHAPTER 17

WELCOME TO WHISTLER

The bellyache had subsided and didn't return for a few days; so, since it had gone away, I wasn't planning to do anything about it. Anyway, I knew there wasn't anything the medical people would do that wouldn't cost me a lot of time and money.

The next weekend arrived and I was ready to get on the road, bellyache or not.

The man grinned as he handed me my change for the five I used to purchase a bottle of water.

I smiled in return waiting for him to speak. It was evident that he had something to say.

"Not from around here, are you?" he said.

"No sir, I'm not."

"I didn't think so. I've never seen you before and I know everyone that lives around here," he said.

"I bet you do," I said as I turned away from the counter.

"Are you lost?" he asked.

I turned back to him and answered, "Well, yes I am. I'm looking for a festival that's supposed to be around here somewhere. The map I printed off the computer wasn't very useful. Could you tell me where Whistler is?"

"Down the road about a mile but I don't know anything about any festival," he said as he scratched the top of his head.

"It's called the Whistler Whistle Stop Festival. It's supposed to be celebrating the days when the passenger trains stopped in Whistler to leave and collect travelers. It's supposed to be set up around the Whistler Train Depot," I explained.

"There ain't never been a train depot in Whistler. The closest railroad tracks are in the next town beyond Whistler. That's about twenty-five miles from here," he said.

I pulled some papers from my handbag and placed them on the counter in front of the perplexed man.

"Where did you get these papers, lady?"

"Off the Internet. I'm a writer and I am constantly looking for places within driving distance of Stillwell to set up a table so I can sell my books. Whistler specifically invited writers to come to set up at their festival."

"This is all lies, lady. Whistler ain't more than about ten houses, not much more than a wide spot on the road."

"Why would it be on the Internet?" I asked.

"Looks like something shady going on to me. I don't think you need to go to Whistler, if you ask me," he said as he shook his head from side to side.

"I don't know. I've come all this way, about ninety miles, over some curvy roads that have led me up and down some pretty good-sized mountains. I really want to see Whistler since I've come this far," I said as I walked out the door to climb back into my car.

I sucked in a deep breath, released it while I was sliding my gearshift into "drive", and took off for Whistler.

It seemed to be a long mile but I finally saw a sign that said:

WELCOME TO WHISTLER
POPULATION 51

I slowed my car so I wouldn't miss any part of Whistler.

I passed a house on the left that was freshly painted, lawn manicured, with glistening window panes.

"Looks good," I mumbled.

The next house was on the right and it was presentable but not nearly as well taken care of as the first house.

House number three was not a house. It was the town hall. At least, that's what the little sign said that was planted in the front lawn.

House number four on the left, was a doctor's office. It was closed up tight with the shades drawn.

The next structure on the right was a modern, new service station with signs in bright yellow with white happy faces as a logo.

I aimed my car for the first set of gas pumps. It was time for me to fill up so this place was as good as any to get the gas.

There was a sign on the pump telling me to pay in advance. I hated those signs even though I knew they had become a necessary evil in this day and time.

I walked inside the building and was surprised to see only one person present in the brightly shining building.

"May I help you?" asked a middle-aged man from behind the sales counter.

"Where is the festival?" I asked as I glanced around me warily.

"Right this way, ma'am," he said as he came out from behind the counter to lead me to a door in the back of the sales area.

I stood my ground. I did not move.

"There isn't a festival back there," I said. "I'm getting out of here."

"I don't think so, ma'am," said another voice.

When I turned to leave there was another man standing behind me. I had not seen him or heard him enter the building.

"What do you want?" I asked angrily.

"Tell me your name," demanded the man who had been behind the counter.

"Why?" I responded timidly.

"I need to know who you are," said the man who had tried to lead me out the back. He had moved back behind the counter again.

"Ellen, Ellen Holcombe," I sputtered.

"You said you are a writer?" questioned the counter man.

"Yes," I said.

"I've never heard of you," he said sarcastically.

"That's why I go to festivals, mister. I want people to know my name so that when they see it on a book, they will buy that book," I explained sternly as I tried to amp up my courage.

The man behind the counter entered something into a laptop computer.

He looked up and told the second man, "She's not the one we want. Let her go."

I took that conversation as a sign for me to leave.

I ran to the car, climbed inside, and locked the car door.

I would be buying my gas somewhere else.

I drove back to the convenience store to talk to the man that had warned me about Whistler.

When I entered the store, there was a young lady behind the counter.

"Where is the middle-aged man that was here earlier today?" I asked excitedly.

"What middle-aged man? I'm the only one who works here in the daytime," said the confused young lady.

"There was a man here, behind the counter. I talked to him. I bought a bottle of water from him."

"Ma'am, I'm the only person who has been behind this counter all day. You must have stopped someplace else," said the irritated young lady.

"I'm sorry for coming on so strong," I sputtered in explanation. "I did talk to a nice man. He grinned a lot and it was a nice grin, a happy grin. He warned me not to go to Whistler. I did go to Whistler anyway and I wanted to tell him what happened when I arrived there."

"That man you described sounds like my dad, Walter, but it can't be him," she said softly.

"Why not?" I asked.

"He's been dead for five years. He died right here in this store. He was shot by a man from Whistler who was trying to rob the place. So - it couldn't have been him."

"Yeah, I guess you're right. I'm sorry that you lost your father. I'm going to fill up my gas tank. I'll be back in to pay you and then be on my way. I won't be selling any books today."

"You said you were going to tell that man about what happened in Whistler. What did happen?" she continued.

"Nothing really, but they seemed to be making money in an unusual way. It seems to me that they are planning to kidnap someone, a writer, and hold him or her for ransom."

"They can't do that. It's against the law," said the young lady.

"It sure is. That's not going to stop them. They tried it with me and when they couldn't find any mention of a bestseller on the Internet, they let me go. I wasn't rich enough for them, thank God."

"Are you all right?" she asked.

"Yes, but I'm going to pump my gas and get out of here. Then, I'm going to keep a good watch on the television news and the newspaper to see if those guys caught them a rich writer. If the law can't figure out who did the kidnapping, I can tell them. Until then, I'm not saying anything to any kind of law figure. I don't want them coming after me. Those guys don't realize that unless you've written a bestseller and are nationally known, writers don't get rich from writing. That's a fact."

I pumped my gas and went back inside the store to pay the young lady.

"Come back, again," she said with a grin. It was the same grin I saw on her father's face.

"I don't think so," I mumbled as walked through the doorway.

CHAPTER 18

WHO'S THERE?

An ambush in the mall and a near kidnapping had me on edge. Anything out of the ordinary was going to get a reaction out of me.

The sound of heavy breathing stopped me.

"Who's there?" I asked the darkness as I turned my body around and around looking for the owner of the sound.

Silence.

It was so dark; the street light was not illuminating the area.

I looked up to the top of the pole where the light should have been and saw dark, black shadows of a metal arm sticking out from the wooden telephone pole.

"Who's there?" I said softly hoping that no one would answer me.

Why I waited so long to pack up and leave the Wise County Fall Festival was a question I couldn't answer other than to say I was trying to sell my books to anyone with the slightest bit of interest.

After all, I was a writer of fiction and nonfiction and I liked to entertain the world with my words of mystery and truth.

Now, I was questioning my reasoning, not to mention my sanity.

I was carrying a load of tote bags containing my crocheting, my writing materials, cold drinks, the tablecloths with metal book stands, and my handbag. I draped all of the totes from my shoulders so I could have a hand free to unlock the car door. The other hand had to pull the cart that held my books along behind me. I had it in my mind that I could just drop everything and defend myself if the need arose, not that I thought I would have that need. I told myself a little old lady in her sixties really shouldn't have to worry about that, you know.

I walked further, straining to hear the heavy breathing, possibly footsteps crunching on the gravel, but it was hard to hear sounds other than the ones I was making myself.

"Not much further," I told myself in reassuring tones. "I can see my car. I'm almost there. Go away and leave me alone."

I never realized how far away I had parked early that morning. I really didn't have a choice when I arrived because all of the early risers had beaten me to the choice parking spots.

"I should have just left everything sitting and brought my car to my table," I mumbled. "That would have been the smart thing to do."

Since the passing of my husband of twenty-five years, I had begun talking to myself. I didn't proclaim that I was crazy, just lonely, and on some days the sound of my own voice was the only human tone I would hear other than the television that played twenty-four hours or until I left the confines of the house for any length of time.

"Thank God," I shouted as I inserted the car key into the lock of the door. I yanked the car door open, reached into the car to unlock the back door, and threw my bags roughly into the car. Next, I lifted the heavy rolling cart filled with the books I didn't sell and placed it on the back seat after shoving the bags out of the way.

I glanced around, searching for the reason for the sounds of danger and the goose bumps that were crawling up and down my plump body.

Crooked Road Stalker

I knew I had to be a sight to see. A gray-haired, overweight woman, jumping into her car and peeling off of the parking lot like she was being chased by the devil himself.

"Get a grip, Ellen," I mumbled as I glanced into my rearview mirror. "You actually didn't see a soul chasing after you. What makes you think someone would want to harm you in any way?"

I glanced into my rearview mirror again and smiled broadly when I saw no glaring headlights following close behind me.

"Was it my imagination?" I asked softly as I pulled my car into my driveway. Again I glanced into my rearview mirror to observe no one or nothing jumping out of the darkness to scare me or even worse.

My imagination led me astray on occasion but deep down in my soul, I really didn't believe it was my imagination this time. The feeling was too strong.

I climbed from the car, slammed the door, and the thought of unloading all of my book paraphernalia flashed through my mind. My only response was to walk directly to my front door and insert the house key. The next morning would be soon enough to unload. I had my fill of the dark, lonely outdoors. It was time to go into the house, turn on all of the lights, and put an end to the real or imagined danger.

Being alone all of the time really sucked; but, like it or not, that was my life. Yes, I had children; two sons to be exact, who had lives and families and obligations that didn't include babysitting mom. Anyway, I was too independent to allow myself to be tied to the house without the freedom to do whatever I wanted whenever I wanted to do it.

Acquiring independence after the break-up of my first marriage from a husband, who didn't love me, helped me become a strong, single woman.

My first husband had proclaimed his love for me, but he had also sought out the company of other women during our marriage.

He blamed his tendency to stray on his drinking.

He married two more times after our divorce and I was happy about those marriages. Strangely enough, wife number two died of a drug overdose and wife number three succumbed to cancer.

Wife number two was a trial for him because he discovered after the "I do's" that she was a drug addict.

Wife number three was a fine lady who helped him recover from the need to drink. Information garnered from my eldest son indicated that wife number three was a good influence and it was a great loss when she died.

At the conclusion of our divorce he had indicated that if he could not have me, he would see to it that no one else did. That statement was made thirty years ago. Would he still mean it today?

"Naw, he should have gotten over it by now," I whispered angrily.

The telephone interrupted my thoughts of bad memories and loneliness. I grabbed for the receiver without bothering to look at the caller ID. I just needed someone to talk to and I was not particular about who was on the other end of the line.

"Mom?" questioned a familiar voice.

"Hi, honey," I said softly with happiness filling me.

"I'm sorry I haven't called sooner but I've been so busy," he hurriedly explained.

"No problem, Aaron. How's Becky?" I asked in a soothing tone as I tried to slow his verbal barrage.

"She's at work. She's okay," he answered.

The conversation didn't last long. It was one of the check-in phone calls that were more obligation than pleasure. I knew I couldn't tell Aaron about my fear of being followed, if that was what was happening. Aaron

71

lived half-way across the country in Nebraska while my home was in Virginia. There was no need to worry him.

As if on cue, the phone jangled again and my eldest son, Eddy, was on the other end.

"Hi, Eddy. I just hung up from talking to your brother," I said brightly.

"How's Aaron doing?" he asked.

"He's fine. Don't the two of you talk to each other?" I asked.

"No, not much. How are you doing, mom?" he said.

I didn't want to tell Eddy that I was afraid of going outside in the dark because some big, ugly ogre was waiting for me.

"Just great, Eddy," I lied.

Both sons had checked in for the month. I didn't expect to hear from them again for several days. Those two boys were my family, my only family. Anyone else that was clinging to the same family tree took no interest in me or what might happen to me.

The lack of concern in my branch of the tree could be traced back to my mother and father. There was never any participation in reunion activities or family gatherings by my parents other than the occasional funeral. I didn't know my relatives and they didn't know me.

If I had a family reunion, it would be really small. Eddy, Aaron, their partners Donna and Becky, and I would be the only ones in attendance to represent my side of the family just like it was at my husband's funeral. If it weren't for the people I worked with, my husband's side of the family would have outnumbered my side by fifty or more.

When my husband's family loaded up and left, I never saw them again. That was a story explained by the fact that I was my husband's second wife and not the mother of his children; thus, I was never accepted and always considered an unwelcome outsider.

The only way I could live with the rejection and dejection was to emphasize my need for independence. Did I really want the world to believe I was so very independent? No, but what choice did I have? The world had seen fit that I was always alone, like it or not.

Going to fairs and festivals weekend after weekend gave me an opportunity to talk to people even if it was only a sales pitch.

Why would anyone want to scare me away from the only real pleasure I had in life?

But, then again, was it for real? Or was it my writer's imagination that had gone out of control?

Perhaps the loneliness made me paranoid, but I didn't believe that, not for a minute.

CHAPTER 19

I LEFT AN HOUR EARLY

During my work week my mind returned many times to my feeling of being watched. Someone was following my every movement, but it only seemed to happen on the weekends when I was peddling my books. Was I really paranoid? Did I have a stalker? Why, in heavens name, would anyone be stalking me, a gray haired woman in her sixties?

I was trying not to arrive too early at my scheduled destinations. In so doing, I felt rushed and out of time. I guess the feeling goes back to the idea taught to me by my father that it was a sin to be late for work, for church, for anything.

I found it so difficult to un-train myself of a good thing.

I arrived at the Historic Crab Orchard Museum and was surprised to find my writer friend, Annie, set up in the area where I thought I was going to display my wares.

More than the disappointment of seeing my set-up space taken, I was hurt by the fact that she didn't tell me she was going to be there. I'm sure that this goes back to my feeling that writers don't want to share the limelight or the possibility of a sale.

I got over the "hurt" quickly. It was the only way to survive and try to maintain the camaraderie that I needed so much.

"Hi, Ellen, I didn't know you were going to be here," Annie said as she tried to tone down her look of surprise.

"Hi, Annie, nice to see you," I said without enthusiasm.

"It was first come first serve, and I got here at 8:30 am. They didn't even open the doors until 9:00 am," Annie explained.

"You can either be in the exhibit gallery or in the hall in front of the gift shop across from the bathrooms," said the professional sounding lady controlling the gift shop and surrounding display areas.

"The hallway and bathrooms; that will be fine," I said as I tried to feign happiness and gratitude.

I made a second trip to my car to unload items for display and then I set out to make my table appealing to the wandering reader.

I seethed a little. I shook it off and remembered to be a lady.

"Ellen, if I buy a blooming onion later, will you share it with me?" she asked.

"Sure, Annie. It's too big for one person to eat. I'd be happy to share one," I answered.

My set-up was ready and I could finally relax.

The crowd was not interested in spending frivolously on anything other than food. No amount of smiling or cajoling was going to get the group, in general, to release the dollars to purchase a nonessential item such as a book.

I watched the people parade in and out, clutching their pockets tightly.

I believe Annie had sold a workbook or two.

Andrew from the Stillwell County Historical Society told me he was having a so-so day.

The economy had damaged us again. I was going to run into that problem all summer long. I was planning ahead for disappointment.

Gracie came by. She didn't have my new nonfiction. I hoped she would come back to buy a copy.

Crooked Road Stalker

The time passed slowly. Gracie came back to buy the only book I sold at the Historic Crab Orchard Museum.

I was scheduled to leave an hour early in order to drive to Jewell Ridge for the Homecoming. I probably missed some sales; at least, that's what Annie told me, but I didn't want to be late for the next book event.

I looked at my windshield.

No note.

I probably left before the note leaver could find my car. I no longer thought it was my ex-husband so I didn't have a clue behind the reasoning of who was trying to scare me.

CHAPTER 20

SO PARANOID

I arrived in a frenzy. I hadn't realized how long the drive to Jewell Ridge was from Stillwell. It took almost an hour and I believe I worried about being late the entire time.

Again, the sweat poured off of me as I unloaded and set-up. It wasn't so hard to unload because the lady who was in charge of the entire homecoming festivities took it upon herself to help me. Sometimes it paid to be a sixty-something woman with gray hair.

I was led to the gymnasium of the old elementary school and given my choice of setting up in the middle of the floor or up against the wall behind some high display panels representing the coal interests in the area.

"We will move these panels if they bother you," said the arts and crafts show director.

My displeasure must have registered on my face. I've been told by my family members that I'm just like my grandmother on my dad's side. She couldn't hide her feelings and I guess I couldn't either. I was glad to be like my grandmother most of the time.

"Leave the panels up. We'll move our table over a bit, if that's okay?" said Andrew who was selling books for the Stillwell County Historical Society.

I shook my head in agreement and went about my business of getting my table set up for presentation to the Jewell Ridge Homecoming attendees.

Crooked Road Stalker

The hours seemed to crawl by because the traffic was slow inside and through the gymnasium. There was an occasional spurt of activity but most buyers hovered around the tables of books offered by the Stillwell County Historical Society. It was good for them; not so good for me. I ended the selling hours by foisting two more of my literary offerings onto the unsuspecting public.

I had hoped to pack up and be gone before the fireworks display started. That didn't happen.

The light rain that had started earlier in the evening didn't dampen the desire for what seemed to be most of the residents on the western end of Stillwell County from watching the large, multi-colored bursts of exploding fire over a cloud darkened, pitch-black sky.

I was sitting in my car to avoid the rain with no hope of moving into a completely stopped traffic flow because the road had become a public parking lot allowing the looky-loos to watch the exploding display.

I was parked, much to my surprise, directly beneath the exploding colors. I leaned forward over my steering wheel and stared straight up. The position was awkward but the fireworks were well worth the little bit of discomfort.

I was disappointed with the sales, or lack of them, but I was pleased with the firework display even though I had become an unwilling on-looker.

From the corner of my eye I caught a glimpse of a hoodie-clad figure standing alone- watching me, I thought.

I reached over to check each of my car doors to see that they were locked. When I returned my glance to where the hoodie-clad figure was standing, he was gone – the hoodie-clad figure was gone. Instead, there was a family cluster standing and staring at the sky.

I was getting so paranoid. Of course, there would be hoodie-clad figures milling around in the darkness.

There was still a fine drizzle falling from the clouds and the hoodie could offer a little protection.

The drive home was long, dark, and lonely. The house was empty except for my three cats and Fred, my dog. I could feel the shadows of depression trying to draw me into their clutches, smothering me with hopelessness and despair.

I cried for me, for Fred, my aging Chihuahua mix dog that was grieving because he missed my husband so very much, and for everyone who ever felt this alone.

CHAPTER 21

A VACATION DAY

It was funny how your mind registered impressions or memories that it determined you should keep fresh in front of any of your future thoughts.

I saw hoodie-clad figures everywhere I traveled during my work week. All of them were being worn by coworkers, friends, or family. I knew they would not be my stalker, at least, that was what I hoped.

Friday arrived and I prepared myself for a trip to The Breaks instead of working for the day at the Stillwell County School Board Office. I had happily chosen to spend a vacation day for the joyful job of selling my books.

I wrestled with my tent, two tables, and all of the paraphernalia required to present my love of writing to the world at the Arts and Crafts Festival that would last for three days.

Ken Hunt, publisher of my fourth book, and writer in his own right, was in a tent next to mine.

Kevin, a creator of decorative Shaker boxes, was on my right side. I felt lucky to be positioned between those two fine gentlemen.

The first day, a Friday, was long and a bit slow. The explanation of the lack of people viewing our wares was that it was Friday and many people were working.

I did manage to sell one book and I was grateful, very grateful, for that lone sale.

I drove for two hours to get home with the hope that Saturday would be better. I paid for my gas only with that one sale. I wanted, at least, to cover my expenses with Saturday sales.

The only saving grace for Saturday was that the park personnel were so nice and apologetic for the lack of buyers.

Two more books were sold and that covered the set-up expenses for coming to The Breaks. I was getting discouraged with the specter of loneliness and depression trying to overtake me again.

One more day at The Breaks, it will be better. I just knew it would. The sagging economy was running rampant over my book sales. Each day had been a success at The Breaks thus far simply because I achieved my goal which was the sale of one book. Above and beyond the one book, I considered gravy.

Sunday arrived and The Breaks was almost over. I drove the two hours without any thought about the sales that might be ahead of me. I had actually wished I had packed up everything the night before and carried it home so I wouldn't have to drive back Sunday. This third day of driving back and forth was going to run me heavily into the red if my sales didn't improve. But, I was committed and I didn't want to think about how much money I was losing.

I reminded myself that, as a writer of the region, I needed exposure. Until my name got recognized, my sales would be sluggish.

I also reminded myself that I appeared in places all weekend long to keep me away from the house and the ever present depression that filled the rooms of my unhappy home.

Sunday that crowd wasn't any larger; not in our part of the park, but they were buying. I managed to sell five more books making my weekend a total success.

When the time came for me to take down the tent and fold up the tables, I was so ready. I was so happy that people were finally beginning to buy my books.

The long trip home didn't seem so tiring. It was funny how a little bit of happiness affected my life.

I unloaded the car so I could repack it for the next trip. I did not inspect anything. I wouldn't do that again until I reloaded for another road trip.

That was a mistake.

CHAPTER 22

WHITE SULPHUR SPRINGS

I unpacked my books, not having looked at them since I left The Breaks.

That was when I found it.

'I'M STILL WATCHING YOU' was written in bright red letters on a note that was stuffed inside one of my books.

Color drained from me and I started shaking.

My stalker, that had to be what he was, was continuing to follow me from festival to festival showing up at each and every one of my book events.

He or she must have stood right in front of me at The Breaks and I didn't know it.

Will my stalker appear before my eyes in White Sulphur Springs, West Virginia?

The people were wonderful, the city was welcoming, and I sold eight books. I was so surprised by that figure because, not being a writer of West Virginia related books, I didn't expect to sell any.

Annie sold more than I did, but I expected her to do so because her books were set in West Virginia. I didn't exactly know how many she sold and I didn't think I should ask. I was not shy about truthfully answering anyone who was interested in my sales. Others weren't quite so free with that information.

Even though the festival in White Sulphur Springs was scheduled for two days, I would only attend the one day because I was going to be at the Virginia Highlands Festival in Abingdon the next day.

This time the drive home wasn't quite so bad. I had kept a keen eye on all of my books and boxes searching for another note to be dropped into or onto my belongings.

When I unloaded the car, I found the note:

SOLD SOME BOOKS TODAY, DIDN'T YOU?

It had been forced into my car through the crack where I had rolled down the window to allow a little air to circulate inside while my vehicle was parked in the hot sun.

Who was doing this? Who was stalking me?

I gathered all of my notes together and placed them in a folder for safe keeping. I was going to visit my friend, J.T. Carter, Sheriff of Stillwell County- maybe.

CHAPTER 23

BRIGHT RED LEGS

During the week, in the middle of my out of town travels, I encountered a medical puzzle that had me a little bit more than just nervous.

The computer had become a necessity in my life because of my writing and the many hours of research that I did. Sometimes the overload of information could cause problems, as was what happened to me.

I sat myself in front of my all-knowing computer and twenty minutes later, after searching over the Internet for what I thought had happened to me, I discovered I could die. Well, maybe I shouldn't be so dramatic, but that's the way I felt about the whole process of finding out what ailed me.

It actually started with my red legs. After staring at those monstrosities for a couple of days, I thought it was best that I take a step towards determining why my normal, but fat, legs had turned bright red from two inches below my knee and encompassing my feet.

Petechia was the name that described the tiny, tiny capillaries and blood vessels that had burst beneath my skin.

I didn't particularly want a label. I wanted it gone.

Then I noticed the bruising. I probably had twenty to thirty dark, ugly, purple marks hidden under my clothing, out of sight, but not out of my mind. The specter of why I was looking as if I had been beaten with a large, heavy instrument hung over me like a shadow.

"My legs have turned red," was the only sensible way of describing the condition.

"Your legs are red?" asked the skeptical medical receptionist.

"Yes," I answered as I tried to control the tone of my voice. I knew she was trying to assess my problem over the telephone as to whether it was an emergency or not.

"What happened to make them red?" asked the young lady as she struggled to keep the need to laugh from her voice.

"That's what I'm trying to find out. I didn't burn my legs and they don't itch or have any visible bumps or rashes. They are red," I said in frustration. "Oh, yeah, and I have a bunch, of big, ugly, purple bruises all over my body. Can I have an appointment with Donna today, if possible?"

"No, not today. Monday is the earliest I can schedule you."

"Okay," I said as she rattled off the available time slot.

It was Wednesday. I would have to wait five days before I could even begin to get an explanation.

Normally, I'm not an alarmist, but I don't get sick very often and I didn't want to be laughed at and brushed off like a piece of lint.

I waited until after lunch and I called the Family Practice Center again asking for Donna, a nurse practitioner, and my dear friend.

"Donna, I think I need to see you before Monday when my appointment is scheduled."

"Sure, Ellen, come on in. I'll fit you in between appointments if you think you really need to see me today."

I felt a little bit of relief after talking to Donna but I knew this problem was not normal. I just didn't know how 'not normal'.

The young ladies at the Family Practice Center each had to come into the room a take a look at my legs.

"I've never seen anything like that," said June.

"Neither have I," added Bessie.

They were no longer laughing about my description of my 'red legs.'

Donna was concerned, not so much about the red legs, but definitely about the bruising.

I had guessed the whole problem was blood related.

Donna had the same idea and ordered six tubes of blood be drawn for lab analysis along with a urine specimen.

Right off, she discovered that I had a urinary tract infection that I didn't know I had.

"What kind of medication do you take?" she asked as she probed for answers.

"Nothing except Ibuprofen for pain and a baby aspirin," I replied.

"Nothing else?" Donna questioned.

"No, I don't like to take medicine. You know that. I don't like to go to the doctor," I explained.

"You're sure you don't take anything else?" she asked again.

"No, why?" I wondered.

"Sometimes reactions to medicine can cause the problems you're having. It could be the Ibuprofen. Stop taking that now. Stop taking any other medication you might be taking," Donna instructed.

"Well, it's not the Ibuprofen. I've taken that on and off for years. I don't take anything else, Donna," I said with irritation evident because I didn't think Donna believed me.

When the blood analysis returned to Donna's office, the low blood platelets waved a bright red flag before Donna's eyes.

"Ellen, I've scheduled you an appointment with a specialist, a hematologist in Richvale. He needs to find out why your platelets are so low," she explained.

The appointment was scheduled for the next afternoon. Talk about fast service, too fast actually. This whole thing was beginning to make me nervous.

Was I sick? I didn't feel sick. I did get tired but I was over sixty years old. Tired comes with age, doesn't it?

I traveled the twenty-mile trip to the specialist alone with my mind running through the possibilities of the illnesses I uncovered on the Internet.

Blood disorders covered a world of reasons, but my mind was afraid of one in particular and that was leukemia. Most of the dead leaves that have fallen off of my family tree have succumbed to cancer in one form or another. I've always felt that would be the reason for my death.

I climbed from the car in the parking lot behind the medical building where the doctor's office was located and proceeded to follow the long narrow hallways searching for Suite 1200.

Just before I arrived at the door to Suite 1200, I noticed a large sign announcing the type of specialized medicine he practiced.

"Welcome to the Oncology Department" was splashed across the wall in bright blue letters.

I stopped suddenly and stared at the sign. I didn't realize I was seeing a doctor in the Cancer Center.

I was scared. I walked slowly to the office door afraid that I might be opening that door to enter into my short and painful future

The doctor never once mentioned leukemia or any specific disease. He assured me that we wouldn't know anything until the lab tests returned.

The specialist asked for eleven tubes of blood to be drawn. With that blood drain accomplished, I was off and running to determine my fate.

"It could be anything," I told my friends and family. "Or, it could be something that can be cured with a pill. That's what I'm hoping. I truly hope a pill can take care of it."

Six days later at a second appointment with the hematologist, I was told I had ITP, idiopathic thrombocytopenic purpura, a blood disorder whose origin was unknown at this point in time. That would be determined with further tests and that I might not be dying after all.

Isn't it funny how your mind can jump to conclusions? Maybe I'm not dying after all. Then again, I could be hit by a car crossing the street.

Twenty minutes and the Internet was all it took to make me feel like I was on my death bed.

CHAPTER 24

THE PARTY THAT NEVER WAS

With having survived the bright red legs, I continued to live my life without too much to worry about except maybe the stupid bellyache that attacked me once in a while. The time span between attacks had stretched out a bit so I didn't worry about it until the pain hit. I would give it ten to twenty minutes to subside and then I would go about my business.

Struggling to my feet, I decided it was time I took a walk. I had been sitting much too long causing my bones and joints to become stiff and difficult to move without pain. That was caused by plain old age and not any kind of undiagnosed God-awful illness.

I was a gray-haired, old woman who lived alone, not that I chose to do so, but only because my husband had passed on several years earlier leaving me to face the sameness of days one after another.

Winter was my nemesis. I couldn't get out of the house to meet and greet people in my tent at festivals of my choosing.

Television watching was my reason for living. It passed the long daylight hours with its set routine from which I did not vary until the darkness arrived and I could go to bed.

I walked to the kitchen to get a can of cat food to open for my kitty cats who were my only daily companions since the decline and death of Fred. I was absolutely sure Fred died because he lost Sonny, his best friend and my husband.

"Come on, babies," I said loudly. "Mommy is going to feed you now."

"Meow," commented Cloudy as she sat next to the newspaper that designated the feeding area. Cloudy was a white cat dappled with clouds of gray. She had bright green eyes and a sweet personality.

"Meow," said Wild Child, a big, big blue gray cat with decorations of white on her nose and feet. She was the niece of Cloudy. She was twice the size of Cloudy, weight wise, and was very demanding of your attention.

Finally, Jughead sidled up next to the girls. He was Cloudy's brother and Wild Child's uncle. He was a black and white beauty with enormous yellow eyes.

All of my kitties were getting old, just like me, and all have been fixed so they can't procreate, just like me.

I finished my daily tasks of cleaning the litter box and searching the refrigerator for food for my own consumption. I decided the few dishes I had in the sink could wait until tomorrow to be washed.

I resumed my job of television watching so my mind was filled with foolishness and dreams that could never be; not in my lifetime, not during what's left of it.

This was only the seventh month of my retirement and I dreaded the thought of years and years left of this way of living.

I had promised myself that I would join clubs for old people, visit hospitals, and write. Obviously I had broken all of those promises.

The writing part was what I should be doing, but why bother. I knew my stories were good but I was not going to be a bestseller. That was not what I had planned to do.

A regional writer, one who was recognized in her small spot in Appalachia, was what I had always dreamed of being. But – in my small spot in Appalachia, people were too busy to read; too busy to give over a few moments of their time; too selfish or jealous, I didn't know which, to support a coworker or friend or family member by making an appearance at a reading or signing of her most recent book release.

In my small part of Appalachia, I was always preparing for a party that never was. I would prepare sweet treats with coffee and cold drinks to welcome some of the two hundred people to whom I had mailed postcards of invitation.

Many times- far too many times- I had packed up my books, sweet treats, hot and cold drinks, and headed for home without one of my books being sold or one of my so-called friends appearing before me to give me a congratulatory hug.

I was afraid that I would while away my days watching television, dreaming about the friends and family I rarely saw, and waiting to die the lonely death that was in my future.

That had always been my fear: dying alone.

That was also why I had my beloved kitties. If they were with me, I was never alone.

Loneliness was the reason that forced me out into the world of the regional writer as I traveled the writing circuit along the Crooked Road each and every weekend during the spring, summer, and fall, if the truth were known by anyone who cared.

My stalker was trying to put an end to my only chance to interact with real live human beings.

I wasn't going to let that happen. I was going to Abingdon to the Virginia Highlands Festival where I could meet and greet people. I would let the world around me know that I was still alive and kicking.

CHAPTER 25

VIRGINIA HIGHLANDS FESTIVAL

A trip of a little bit less than an hour and a half was going to take me to my next location for book sales. The Virginia Highlands Festival in Abingdon was my next stop on my writing circuit.

The moment I jumped into my car, the rain started. I was so glad I had packed the car with my books the night before.

The rain was sporadic in intensity. For one stretch of road, there were the lightest of sprinkles followed by another section being pelted with drops so big and so heavy I couldn't see what was in front of me.

With great foreboding, I unloaded my car at the big tent the festival leaders had provided and prepared for a long, wet day.

We had to keep everything that could be damaged by water up off the pavement. Of course, that didn't include my feet and they stayed wet and cold for the entire day.

There were a few brave souls running from tent to tent, but the crowd was sparse. I couldn't blame the public for not wanting to wander around in the rain, dodging the raindrops from tent to tent seeking a dry spot.

About mid-afternoon, I sold a book. Boy, was I surprised and thankful for the lady making my day a success.

Late afternoon finally brought out the Sunday sunshine with predictions for a much dryer Monday.

With arrival of Monday morning, I prepared to drive to Abingdon, again, rather than go to my busy job at the Stillwell School board Office.

That was my first time trying to sell books on a weekday at the Virginia Highlands Festival. My hope was that I would exceed the sale of the previous day that only amounted to one book.

I was happily surprised with the sale of four books making the bright, sunshiny day a wonderful change.

I returned to Abingdon and the big tent on the following weekend.

If anyone was out to get me, I would be easy enough to find especially since I sent news releases to all of the local newspapers announcing my appearances.

It was a hot, humid day.

"Rodney, you're looking a little flushed," I said as I watched my booth mate closely.

"I'm feeling a little dizzy and I've got a headache," he explained as he rubbed his hands over his face.

"Sit here for a few minutes. I'll get a cold cloth to hold against the back of your neck. Then, I think you should go on home. The heat is really getting to you," I instructed.

I ran to the hand washing station where I grabbed a few paper towels and placed them under the water that I pumped from the reservoir with my foot.

Rodney held the towels in place for a few moments before the red drained from his face.

"Rodney, you've cooled off enough, I think, so you can drive home. I'll help you pack your books and walk you out to your car. You should be okay to drive for a short distance. Email me later to let me know you're okay," I said.

I wasn't happy about being the only one left in the booth but I was under a large tent filled with other booths and vendors. I wasn't completely alone.

I was talking to some potential customers when I noticed that sides were being dropped on the large tent. My customers scurried out and I discovered I was alone, again. All of the other vendors had been ready and waiting for the sides to drop.

They were gone.

"Oh, God, I've got to get out of here," I prayed.

I packed my books into the case with wheels, grabbed my many tote bags, and placed my car keys in my hand ready to be thrust forward to the lock on my car door.

I didn't look around to find out if I was being followed. I really didn't want to know. I focused my eyes straight ahead and walked directly to my car where I dropped everything to the ground to free my arms of the burden of totes.

I had that feeling again.

I was standing beside my car when I saw a man approaching me. I prepared myself to run by kicking the totes out of my path.

"Ellen, is that you?" asked a somewhat familiar voice.

I whirled around to see my first husband standing in front of me.

"What do you want?" I asked harshly. "Have you been following me?"

"Yes, but I was trying to find the best way to approach you. I know you don't ever want to see me again," he explained.

"You're right, get out of here!" I shouted trying to hide the fact that I was scared.

"I'm dying, Ellen. I just want to make things right with us," he continued.

"Okay, you've done that. Now go," I said without sympathy.

I watched him turn to leave. I wanted to say I'm sorry but I would not allow myself to do so. It would only stir up some bad memories that were better off forgotten and allowed to die, finally, with husband number one. He continued to walk away and I loaded my car with my scattered belongings. It was hard to lose this husband, too, especially for a second time. The first time was bad enough with me having to live through a divorce that felt like a death to me.

Husband number one was gone forever, hopefully, I thought as I brushed the tears from my cheeks.

Was he my stalker?

My gut told me my ex wasn't the person following me. My heart told me I should have been nicer to him.

"Maybe I'll call him later and explain that I was frightened; then again, maybe I won't. I don't want to stir up feelings that are best left alone," I mumbled as I drove home in the dark of night.

I actually didn't notice whether or not there was a hoodie-clad figure near my car.

Maybe that was a good thing.

CHAPTER 26

NOON SHOW AND IN FOCUS

My next excursion out of town was going to take me to the local television station about twenty-five miles away to make a brief appearance on the Noon Show.

I was going to have to leave work at eleven in the morning, drive for a half hour to arrive at the television station by eleven-thirty so I could talk to Steffie Harris before the live broadcast. She wanted to make sure I would be able to speak in front of the camera without creating any embarrassment for either of us.

Steffie was a tall, elegant, black lady who oozed with refinement. She almost appeared snooty, but I could be wrong. Unfortunately, I discovered she was leaving the station by attaining a job where there is a much larger audience in Charlottesville. I wasn't told this information directly. I just picked up on it through overheard conversations.

I didn't tell anyone at work that I was going to be on the Noon Show because I wanted to slip out and get back without anyone questioning me about my taking a two-hour lunch break.

The camera didn't make me uncomfortable. It wasn't like talking to a room filled with attentive people. There were four people present on the news set; Steffie, the weather man, the camera man, and me.

My next foray into the world of publicity was to tape an episode of "In Focus" for the local television station. They offered that public service to people with something to say from the region.

Fortunately, they thought that a local author deserved some free publicity. I was glad they felt that way. I certainly would not be able to pay for that kind of air time.

I was usually a little nervous when the one-on-one interview started, but when I began talking about my books, the anxiety left me. My books were part of me and I was like a proud mother showing off her offspring.

The interviewer was the same young lady that I had met six months earlier. I was comfortable with both her and her questions so what little nervousness I felt soon dissipated.

Asking about my books and my love of writing always put me at ease.

I walked out of the building that housed the television station into the lighted area that led to the darkened parking lot.

Before I left the lighted area, I glanced around slowly to see if a hoodie-clad figure was sitting in a car – waiting.

"Good, no strangers," I whispered as I ran to my parked car so I could drive home to the safety of my little house.

CHAPTER 27

THE WRITERS' GROUP

In an effort to fill up time and meet new people, I searched for and found a group of writers who allowed me to join their little circle of friendship. It felt really great to be a part of something.

Until I stumbled across an article about him in the paper, I never realized how much Walter Dodge and I were alike, I thought, as I gazed at the officer standing in front of me with notepad in hand.

"We didn't look like each other physically, but we traveled many times in the same circles and participated in the same events so often that we became close enough to call each other by our first name and pull each other into a friendly hug on sight.

"I'm getting ahead of myself in this story. We need to go back, don't we, Officer? We need to get to the part where his path and mine split."

"Yes ma'am, we need to know a little about his background. Everyone around here tells me you are the one to talk to. Is that right, ma'am?"

"I guess so. No one else particularly cares about either one of us. We have or had, both of us, each lost a spouse. I think that common tragedy was the basis of the attraction, if you want to call it that – attraction, I mean."

"What can you tell me about his personal life?" the officer asked.

"Like what?" I demanded. I was not liking this type of questioning and I wanted the officer to know exactly how I felt.

"Well, ma'am, who were his close friends?" he questioned further.

"I don't have any idea. I just know him, or I should say knew him, from the writers' group. We had no personal relationship, officer."

"Can you tell me anything about his friends?" the officer asked.

"As far as I know, his friends were my friends and vice-versa," I replied.

"Of the friends that you and he had, can you tell me if any them had a problem with Walter Dodge?" the officer continued.

"Have you ever known any writers, officer?" I asked.

"I can't say that I have, ma'am," he answered sheepishly.

"Writers are a different breed, officer. Some of us are willing to share thoughts and ideas about what we do and who we know. The majority of us, however, are very, very territorial. The only thing we are willing to share will cost you the price of a book."

"Are you one of those territorial writers?" he asked.

"No officer, I'm not. I just want you to know that you might find it difficult to get information from some of the others in the group."

"You didn't answer my question, ma'am," said the officer in an attempt to steer the conversation to where the answers were pertinent.

"I'm sorry, what was the question again?" I asked in frustration.

"Do any of your friends that you shared with Walter Dodge have a problem with him?" he repeated.

"No sir, but Walter wasn't an easy person to get along with most of the time," I answered.

"Why would you say that?" he probed.

"He tended to be aloof, stand-offish, peering down at everyone like he was better than whomever it was he was conversing with at that particular moment. He was only of average height but his holier than thou demeanor made him appear to be a towering giant who didn't approve of anyone other than himself," I explained.

"You didn't like him, did you?" the officer continued with the questioning.

"Not especially. Like I said, we were thrown together because of common loss."

"Did he treat everyone the same way in the writers group?" he asked.

"I can't speak for everyone else, but I couldn't see any difference from one person to another."

"Do you have anything else you can add, Mrs. Holcombe?" he asked with finality.

"No sir."

"Take my card and if you can think of anything to add, please call," he said as he handed me his business card.

"I thought he killed himself, officer. Why are you questioning people like we are all suspects in a murder?"

"We investigate all deaths, ma'am, even suicides," with that revelation, Officer Martin walked away to question other members of the writers' group.

Walter Dodge was a pompous, vain, egotistical, older man with visions of his own grandeur. His average height carried his extra poundage well and his almost white crop of hair and manicured moustache attracted the older ladies, especially from my generation.

His acceptable good looks were where the attraction was likely to end. Once he opened his mouth and spoke to them in his condescending tone, they shied away from him.

I didn't tell the investigating officer, but I thought everyone in the writers' group, at one time or another, wished Walter Dodge dead. But – why throw dirt on a dead man?

Walter was the president of the writers' group and with that title came the right, he thought, for him to berate the underlings. He was rapidly running off the writers because of his attitude. The only reason he was elected to president was because no one else wanted the job that had many responsibilities attached.

In other words, we brought it on ourselves by being apathetic and lazy; foisting the job onto the only one willing to take it.

The officer said the death of Walter Dodge was being investigated as a homicide but I truly think it was a suicide. If I had the same opinion of the world that Walter Dodge had, I probably would have killed myself, too.

I did have his outlook and dread, but I got over it.

I accepted the imperfect world full of imperfect people, of course, that included me and I moved on. Walter Dodge couldn't do that and Walter Dodge died at his own hand rather than accept life as he was living it.

The death of Walter Dodge gave all of the writers who knew him material for writing. To the writers, he may not have been useful in life, but his death will be written about by each and every one of us in one way or another.

This writing was proof of that.

My mind wandered back to my stalker. Did Walter Dodge have a stalker?

No – I didn't think so.

I'm sure he wouldn't have known it if he did. No one would dare, in Walter's opinion, cause him bodily harm.

CHAPTER 28

LEMONADE DAYS

I was sinking down into a bad funk, a depression that I really needed to shake off.

Again, I was taking a vacation day from work, except this time it was a last minute decision. I called on Tuesday morning to check on the availability of space for me to sell my books. I really didn't think it would be a problem, but I thought it best to ask.

Friday arrived and I was headed to Bluefield, Virginia, for Lemonade Days.

Bluefield called itself the "nature's air-conditioned city." That was to say the two Bluefields said that. Even though Bluefield, Virginia, was classified a town, because of its borders with Bluefield, West Virginia, a city, it was included in that air-conditioned city classification.

Since the early 1940's if the temperature reached 90 degrees, the two Bluefields served lemonade free of charge to any and all takers in certain specified areas of the Bluefields.

This was only the second year of the festival of Lemonade Days in Bluefield, Virginia, so I knew there wasn't going to be a huge crowd.

I sold one book.

The day wasn't a loss by any means.

I didn't find a note.

I didn't see a hoodie-clad figure.

Maybe I had outsmarted my stalker by making a sudden last minute decision to sell my books at Lemonade Days.

Maybe he had succeeded in what he wanted to do and that was to make me ever vigilant and paranoid.

I knew for a fact that I had become much more careful when traveling and living alone.

At home, I usually kept all of my doors locked. I opened the big heavy door to allow the sun to enter and chase away the darkness, but I kept the storm door latched and locked to keep away unwelcome visitors.

Maybe it was a good thing to be stalked – no – no way was it good.

CHAPTER 29

PICCADILLY

During the long winter months, I tried to visit some of the restaurants within driving distance where I could set up a table in the lobby to sell my books.

One of those restaurants that allowed me to sell my books was the Piccadilly.

I was going to be people watching for a period of nine hours and counting.

A distinguished gentleman, with white hair, a ramrod straight back, and impeccable eating habits was sitting at a table to my left. He glanced at me and I at him. Our eyes caught for a moment and I could feel a flush of embarrassment.

A young couple with two young boys was also to my left where one of the boys was eating mashed potatoes with his fingers and spreading the excess over the seat and back of the booth. His younger brother was screaming merely because it was fun to make that kind of disruptive racket.

Today was the day for eaters who were dining alone with the majority of them being gray and white-haired ladies. I used to think I would rather miss the meal than to have to sit in a booth by myself consuming a meal that became tasteless and bland for the lack of good company.

My opinion changed over the last few months. I've had to face facts. I was alone from daylight to dark with only coworkers popping in and out of my life during the day until I finally retired.

My cats, Cloudy, Jughead, their mama Shadow, and her grand kitty, Wild Child, were the entities that filled my evenings trying to chase away the loneliness of missing my beloved Sonny. Most of the time I accepted the unconditional love that my animals had to offer, but once in a while it wasn't enough.

The only way I could drive away the pain was with loud, gut-wrenching sobs, followed by my slamming and banging a couple of drawers so I could release the pent-up pressure.

Then – I went to bed.

I tried to sleep away the depression, the loneliness, and the shame of being so very weak.

Most people in the Piccadilly walked by my table without a glance or with their eyes averted to avoid my enticing eye contact.

Two people had hurriedly made a purchase as they were exiting the cafeteria thereby making my day a success.

I had my cell phone with me, but it never rang. My son, the one who lived locally, never remembered the number so if he wanted to call me, he left a message on my home phone. I was not sure if my other son, who lived in Nebraska, knew my cell number.

Not many other people who filled my life even knew I had a cell phone. And, of course, I didn't have a man in my life since the death of Sonny. I was not sure I was ready to cross that bridge yet. I was not searching for a replacement for Sonny.

The fact that I jumped at the chance to cancel the only date that I had had since Sonny died ten months ago told me that I wasn't ready – not yet.

My friend, Patty, had talked me into accepting a blind date with a widower close friend of her and her husband, Randy.

"He's really a nice man, Ellen. His wife died a couple of years ago and I've talked him into dating again."

"I don't know, Patty."

"It's time, Ellen. You know that and he is such a nice man. He's the one that built our house. But – I need to tell you that he is eighty years old."

"Patty, I don't want to watch another man die," I whispered softly.

"Don't worry, Ellen. He is not ready to die. He is sharp as a tack and healthy as a horse. I promise you, Ellen. He isn't going to die."

"I don't know, Patty."

"Just think about it, Ellen."

"I will," I said as I hung up the telephone.

"God, how I hate weekends," I mumbled as I struggled to get through the long Friday workday.

There was once a time when all I did was live for the weekends praying that the routine, time stealing weekdays would hurry up and pass through the hours. I wished my life away when I was younger always wishing for the weekend to appear sooner rather than later.

Now, I knew what I had to face each and every weekend. It was the same fate I confronted each evening after I arrived home from work.

Alone – I was always alone.

The death of my husband brought with it the death of my life as I once lived it.

I was still learning to be so completely alone.

This weekend might be a little different. Last Friday I went home after work and I never left the house until I returned to work Monday morning. I did the routine weekly cleaning, washing of clothes, writing checks to pay bills, and crying a lot.

That was what I had done for the last several months. I cried a lot and spent hour after hour alone unless

I was at work where I actually had face to face human contact.

This weekend I had managed to schedule a book signing to promote my newest mystery novel. Needless to say, I was a writer.

I was truly fed up with this, this feeling sorry for myself. 'I have got to get a life' was my new mantra that I chanted when I was sinking down, down to the darkness.

Friday arrived and so did the flow of tears. They had been pent up all week because of the break in boredom by the ten to twelve hours I spent at the office daily. I only got paid for working eight hours but that was fine with me. I just wanted to get out of the house, away from the three cats that seemed to feel they owned the house and everyone and everything in it.

I had a lady friend who called me every night since the death of Sonny. I had another friend that called me every morning at the same time to begin my day.

I looked forward to both of those telephone calls. I was sure my friends didn't know how much I needed those calls.

The next work day I awoke in a foul mood that seemed to be determined to hang onto me for the entire day and evening. I knew it was there because I was even considering spending time with a man other than Sonny. I had put myself on a guilt trip. That was a stupid move, I know, but I was there. My mind wouldn't accept the fact that I would not be cheating on Sonny.

I talked with a couple of coworkers who encouraged me to take a chance and when Patty called again, I said yes.

Patty was so excited she called the gentleman and gave him my phone number. Less than an hour later he was on the other end of my telephone line.

"Ellen, this is Gary Bowman, Patty's friend.

"Hi, Gary," was all I managed to get out without a struggle. It has been such a long time since I had had a one-on-one conversation with a man with intentions of getting to know me personally.

"Patty says we should get to know each other," said Gary.

"Sounds good to me," I said hoping not to sound too interested.

"I've known Patty for a number of years. I've done some work for them. I sold them the two log structures they built at Claypool Hill and I've done a lot of work on their new house," he explained in rapid words.

"Yes, Patty told me she has known you for a long time."

"I hear you like to write," he said as he struggled to find a subject to talk about.

That was a bingo; just the right comment to make.

"Yes, I've published four books. I have three more ready to publish and I'm working on three more."

"You're a busy lady," he said softly.

"Yes sir, I am," I said boldly.

"Do you think you can fit in a dinner with me, say Friday evening?" he asked.

"Yes, Friday would be the only day. I'll be busy Saturday in Bristol and Sunday at the West Virginia State Fair with my son and his girlfriend."

"Friday is the only good evening for me, too. My son will be visiting this weekend," Gary added. "I don't know much about good places to eat. I just know where to eat what I like such as Ryan's."

"I like Ryan's, too."

"Good, that's settled. Now what time?" he asked almost gruffly.

"I get off work at three-thirty Friday afternoon."

"How about four-thirty? We'll have an early dinner and avoid the crowds," he added hastily.

"That's good," I said as skepticism filled me.

"Where do you live?" he barked at me.

I gave him my address and it was on. He would pick me up for an actual date; something I hadn't done for twenty-five plus years.

I could feel shadows of depression dancing before me but I fought hard to chase them away.

I stayed busy, keeping my mind occupied so I wouldn't dwell on my decision.

Thursday morning I called the town water department to complain about the fact that my water bill had doubled in cost from the previous month.

"We'll get someone to check your meter, ma'am," said Billie the nice lady at the town hall.

They checked it and, of course, I had a water leak.

"The men are at your house now. Do you want me to have them turn off your water until you get it fixed?"

"No, no, I've got to have my water," I sputtered. "Do you know anyone who can fix it? This is something my husband would normally take care of but he died last November."

"I'm sorry, ma'am. I really don't know anyone."

"Thanks," I said as I hung up the phone.

I called the husband of a friend to see if he knew anyone I could get to do the work for me. He had had recent water problems at the laundry center he owned.

"The guy that did my work charged me an arm and a leg. You wouldn't want him, Ellen."

After I hung up from that conversation, my phone rang immediately.

"This is Billie from the water department. You said you needed someone to find the water leak for you."

"Yes ma'am, I sure do."

"Our meter reader, William Akers, said he would help you find the leak. I'll give you his cell number so you can call him and set up a time."

"Thanks, thank you so much," I gushed into the phone.

110

I called William Akers and he told me he would meet me between three-thirty and four at my house.

William and his young helper walked around outside the house searching for the leak without any luck. I gave them the key to the crawl space under the house and, lo and behold, it was there at the front of house under the flower bed.

My tall, almost blooming sunflowers were going to be destroyed because the ground beneath them had to be dug up to locate the broken pipe.

They consented to do the work the next evening for the quoted price of one hundred and fifty dollars.

The price surprised me. I expected it to be much higher.

As soon as the men left, I went into the house and called Gary to cancel our date.

He didn't answer the phone so I left a message, "Gary, I have a water leak at my house and the men are coming to my house tomorrow evening to fix it. I have to be here so I'm going to have to cancel our date. Is it possible to reschedule? I'm really sorry about this."

I wasn't sure if that last sentence was true or not. Was I really sorry?

Gary called later that evening and we discovered that a new date and time would have to wait for at least a week because I was already tied up with book events.

Would he call again? I didn't know.

I knew that after the pipe repairs had been made, I was alone again. And to think – I could have had a nice meal with a fine gentleman at Ryan's.

Now, I am sitting at the Piccadilly Cafeteria writing on my next book, smiling when required at the passersby as I hoped they wanted to stop and, at least, look at my books.

Two ladies to my left had hairdos from the big hair period of the eighties. They were obvious bottle blondes with the perky up-dos portraying the choice of the time period long past. Their faces did not reflect the youthful appearance of their hair. I believed they were sisters with both ladies refusing to believe they were getting older.

Both ladies were thin as rails, sickly looking, but stopped to speak as they left the restaurant.

People were pleasant at the Piccadilly. Many wished me great success with my writing and selling.

Eight brave souls actually bought books.

Thank you so much for making my day.

Thank you so much for not leaving me a note and scaring me again before my long, lonely drive home.

CHAPTER 30

HEY, WHAT ARE YOU DOING?

Every year since I discovered its existence, I would sign up to go to the Better Living Show, at the Brushfork Armory, in Bluefield, West Virginia. It cost a little more than the other shows that I paid for, but I liked it, so I would come up with the money. I would be placed in the mezzanine with the crafters and other writers like me.

Many of us in the special places up in the rafters of the enormous building got to be friends who looked forward to seeing each other every year.

It was a pain getting up and down the steps to unload and load up again, but if the young college students were around, they could be talked into helping a little old, gray-haired lady. Of course, I paid each one of them for the help when they would or could accept it, so they were willing helpers.

I would be there for very long hours on Friday, 10 am to 8 pm, with the shorter hours of 10 am to 6 pm on Saturday.

By the time 8 pm finally arrived on Friday, I was so ready to go home. It would be a forty-five-minute drive and I could feel my bed calling me but my mind replayed my scare of the day.

"Hey, what are you doing?" I screamed at the dark, hoodie-clad figure standing next to my car.

I tried to propel my sixty-something, overweight body forward, faster, as I aimed myself towards what appeared to me to be a vandal.

The dark, hoodie-clad figure spun around facing me but I was still too far away to be able to distinguish the features of the face that were surrounded by a black hood attached to a sweatshirt. The dark, hoodie-clad figure stiffened with the sound of my footfalls hitting the pavement. My blood curdling scream had no effect on him whatsoever but the sound of my shoes slapping the asphalt caused a quick reaction.

Then – the dark, hoodie-clad figure was gone.

The disappearing was so fast that it seemed like it was magic.

I slowed myself from an almost run to a walk for the final few feet required to reach my car. My eyes traveled all over the driver side of my vehicle searching for some unknown destruction.

There was no damage to be found on my car. I must have interrupted him before he could accomplish his task and that's assuming it was a 'he'.

If I could have parked closer to my assigned booth space, I would have, but when I set up at fairs and festivals, the parking was always haphazard.

Since the death of my husband several months before, I had become somewhat paranoid. It was not that I was afraid because I was not afraid, or at least, I hadn't been until events like the disappearing dark, hoodie-clad figure started occurring.

Of course, my so-called friends told me it was my writer's imagination running wild. I didn't think so, but there was no way I could prove it.

Why would anyone want to harass me? I didn't have a clue. The only person who had posed a threat to me did so more than thirty years ago. I was sure that threat was dead and gone and perhaps the person who hurled threatening words at me might even be no longer among the living.

Other than him and the ugly divorce we endured, I really haven't lived a life that would have attracted to me a group of ill-wishers.

My goal in life was to write and entertain those who might be interested in reading my humble words.

Of course, as with most writers, I wrote about what I knew which made it quite possible for anyone I had ever known during my sixty-plus years to appear on my written pages. Good, bad, or indifferent, you could become one of my characters.

Perhaps one of those people didn't like what I had written about him or her. But who?

The dark, hoodie-clad figure appeared lithe and young, not of my age bracket, so I didn't think it would be from my past life characters unless, of course, it was a child or grandchild of the thought to be wronged person.

No, no, again, I didn't think so.

I grabbed the box of books I had come to fetch out of my back seat and walked back to my table carrying the heavy load up the long staircase.

I spent the day pre-occupied with looking for the dark, hoodie-clad figure and worrying about whether or not he would return to my parked car to finish whatever it was that my appearance had interrupted.

My eyes constantly scanned the ever present steady stream of onlookers. I was looking for the dark, hoodie-clad figure that was emblazoned in my mind, but my rational self told me that that very same dark, hoodie-clad figure could have changed his appearance by simply removing the hooded sweatshirt.

"Ellen, how are you?" asked an acquaintance for whom I was searching my memory for a name. That happened to me a lot. I recognized the face, but the name did not easily leap to mind. I couldn't blame that on getting older because I had always had that problem.

"Hi, I'm fine. How are you?" I responded trying to cover up my ignorance as my mind raced through the faces collected in my past. Then it clicked in, "Nancy, how is the family?"

"Doing well, Ellen, and yours?"

"It's just me now. My husband passed away some time ago, But, I think I have managed to get beyond the devastating hurt," I said.

"I'm so sorry, I didn't know," she said in the phony tone that I had heard a million times from people who were trying to pay lip service for a pain that they couldn't really imagine.

"Well, tell me, are the kids still in the area or have they moved away like one of my boys who now lives in Nebraska?" I asked.

"They are still around for now, but that can change with the economy. Well, it was nice seeing you again, Ellen," she said as she hurried away from my probing questions.

I gazed down the road continuing to search the crowd.

I felt a presence.

I turned my gaze to a dark, hoodie-clad figure standing directly in front of my table.

I could feel my face drain of color.

"Are you all right, Ellen?" asked a familiar voice whose face was obscured by the extremely bright sunlight positioned directly behind the dark, hoodie-clad figure.

I raised my hands to shade my eyes from the glare.

"David, is that you? I can't see you for the sun," I said as I squinted to get a better look.

"Yes, yes, are you okay? You look like you've seen a ghost," said David.

"I thought I had, but it was only you." I replied with a smile as I felt the fear drain away for the moment.

"Thanks a lot, Ellen," he said in a feigned hurt tone.

"You know I didn't mean it that way, David. I'm always glad to see you," I said in a happy tone. "I thought you were someone else, that's all."

"Your reaction tells me it was someone you don't want to see. Am I right?" he asked.

"Yes and no," I answered vaguely.

"Go on," he pushed.

"I saw a dark, hoodie-clad figure standing next to my car when I went to get some books from the back seat. I was afraid he was trying to do something bad like keying my car or even trying to hurt me but he disappeared so quickly I couldn't get a good look at him if it was a him."

"Maybe he was just lost or was checking to see if he had the right car. I'm sure you've walked up to the wrong car thinking it was yours, haven't you?"

"Yes, of course, but his reaction spoke volumes to me about a nefarious deed not of someone being lost," I explained.

"You might be right, but I hope not, Ellen. Do you want me to wait around and help you pack up and leave?" asked David.

"No, David, I'll be fine. There are plenty of people around to help me if I think there will be any trouble."

Of course, I would tell him I didn't need any help. I didn't want him to think I was a helpless wimp. I wanted him to always see me as the strong, independent woman that I was.

Oh, how I wished he would stay and keep me company.

I had met David at the Bluefield Autumn Jamboree.

It was a beautiful morning with a slight chill in the air. I packed the car the night before so I wouldn't have to haul it all out first thing this morning. It was hard enough to handle everything twice a day with the unloading at the site and loading again at the end of the day.

It took me a while to find someone to tell me where to set up; then, I had to figure out how to get my car past all of the road blocks to unload. Luckily I knew that if I made a right turn next to the church and drove around to the back, I would find an alley that would, at least, get me closer to where I needed to go.

There it was. I popped the trunk and pulled out the rolling containers that held my books.

A gentleman, several years younger than me, volunteered to help. I shared the task with him until he was called away by a possible customer at his table.

The helping me duties were taken over by a man, a little older than me, say over sixty, and I was grateful.

I had seen this gentleman several times in the past at festivals but I never actually knew his name until that day.

"My name is David," he said as he extended his hand.

"I'm Ellen," I said as I gratefully shook his hand.

I watched David walk away towards the crowd of people gathering around the musical stage where the bluegrass band would get the crowd stirred up and moving around in happy dancing on the main floor.

I liked David a lot, but I was afraid to take the next step. I lost two husbands from divorce and one from death. I didn't know if I could live though another devastating loss.

It was almost 8 pm. The day was fading along with the light so I started my job of packing up. I wanted to make sure I was not the last one to leave. There was safety in numbers, right?

I was struggling with my load of totes and a wheeled cart, paying no mind to my surroundings. I shoved my last tote containing my binder and writing paraphernalia onto the back seat, stepped back, and bumped into someone standing directly in my path.

I would have said "pardon me" but I was too scared. The words never came to mind neither did the scream that I wanted to emit.

"Are you Ellen Holcombe?" asked a voice from behind me.

I stepped forward towards my car as far as I could go so I could turn and face the body belonging to the voice.

"Who are you? What were you doing to my car?" I demanded.

"I'm Roger, Roger Anders. Someone told me it was your car so I was waiting for you. Would you sign my book? My mother's a fan of yours. I bought her your book at a yard sale. It's the only one she doesn't have. I want to give it to her tomorrow for her birthday."

"Yes, sure," I answered as I watched the dark, hoodie-clad figure standing before me.

"I don't think I will ever get used to having fans," I mumbled with a sigh and a smile.

I prayed I would not be bothered by another dark, hoodie-clad figure.

A fan? Was my dark, hoodie-clad figure a fan?

Before I pulled out of the parking area, I checked for a note tucked under my windshield.

No note.

I walked completely around my car looking for damage or some sign that would tell me my stalker was with me.

I was parked under a light so I could see, just barely, the words scrawled in white chalk on the pavement outside the driver side of my car:

HI, ELLEN!

"God, please help me figure out why he is doing this," I prayed as I jumped into my car and sped away with fear rising up again forcing me to take a deep breath to clear my thoughts.

CHAPTER 31

BINDER OF SECRETS

In among my totes that I would load into my car for each book signing was a special bag that held my binder.

I had searched high and low for the missing binder and was starting to panic. It wasn't that the binder contained anything of monetary value, because it didn't. Then again, maybe it did hold a value that I would not dream of cashing in on other than to use its contents as a basis for future fiction stories I might write.

The contents of the binder were truths I had gathered over the years for my eyes only.

I was a collector, obviously, but my collections were of thoughts and memories. I had filled many notebooks and binders with the idea of using some or all of them eventually on the premise that truth, in many cases, was stranger than fiction.

My binder of truths was so precious to me. It was the only one of its kind in my many different collections that I amassed in my little home.

I didn't hide the names of those involved in the truths so many untold stories were out of my hands circulating in a world that might react with violence and destruction.

What was I thinking when I left it laying around in plain sight?

Then my mind wandered back to the dark, hoodie-clad figure that kept appearing in my life. Would he have taken my binder? If so, why?

Linda Hudson Hoagland

My binder held secrets but, hopefully, I was the only person who could interpret the words I had scrawled out as memory reminders.

Again, my writer's imagination was working overtime, I hoped.

I hadn't noticed my binder was missing until I arrived home and unloaded my car after setting up at the Brushfork Armory.

I knew I had not inadvertently left it setting because I double-checked for a forgotten one, any forgotten one, when I gathered up my remaining totes.

Hours, days, weeks, months, and years had gone into filling that binder with thoughts and ideas for future writings. There was no way possible for me to remember most of what I had jotted down on paper.

"No, Ellen, forget about it. It will show up eventually," I said to reassure myself that I had merely misplaced the tote containing the binder.

CHAPTER 32

ALL SEASONS INDOOR MARKET

Winter was approaching rapidly and that would mean I would be sitting at the house seven days a week until April of the next year with only an occasional excursion out amongst the populace to do a book signing.

Because I had retired from the school board office and the daily grind of working, I found myself, once again, worrying about vegetating.

I was one of those people who needed a reason to get up out of bed every day. Writing alone wasn't going to make me do that.

Don't get me wrong, I loved to write but I knew that couldn't be my only reason for facing each day. I had discovered long ago, that I would write many more words if I had to fight the clock to fit them onto a piece of paper.

Strangely enough, the struggle kept my thoughts clearer, more focused, and ready to jump off my pen.

My friend, David, had told me about the All Seasons Indoor Market located about five miles out of Stillwell. It was a place for vendors, like me and him, where we could go rent a warm, dry space to sell our wares.

I wasn't so much interested in working hard to sell my books and whatever else I decided to display. I was interested in the fact that there would be people milling around at all times.

I wouldn't be alone, that was what I was looking for, plus the fact that it gave me a reason to get up every day for those three days, at least.

I rented a booth. It didn't take me long to make that decision. For the winter, it was what I needed.

With the decision made and the rent paid for the month of January, my thoughts wandered back to my stalker. Would he find me? Would I finally find out his identity? Was it a he?

The months of November and December were always long, miserable months for me to endure since my husband's death.

He died on November 3rd, which was the day before my sixtieth birthday on November 4th.

I was still numb from the loss during the first holiday season after his death. The second year was when I really felt the pain of his loss and what it meant for the holidays.

This was my fifth holiday season of remembering Sonny's death and it was a little easier to live through but I was still glad it was over. As soon as the evening of Christmas Day arrived, I took down the few decorations I had on display and felt good about facing the New Year. The dread of Thanksgiving and Christmas had passed, once again, and now I could go on living. I had yet to figure out how not to be depressed during the holiday season but I found out with the passing of each year, I didn't go down that deep hole of depression quite as far.

Believe it or not, I was looking forward to the arrival of January with its cold weather and snow. I was starting my new job as a vendor at the All Season Indoor Market.

I had managed to move a couple of small loads of stuff to be sold from my booth that was rented mainly for a place to sell my books. The booth was large enough to allow me to clean out my closets and storage building a little at a time just to keep the rent paid.

The last weekend in December allowed me to get everything set up and ready to sell on my first day of receiving the public- that was New Year's Eve Day.

Because it was so soon after the Christmas season, I wasn't expecting to do much selling but I was surprised with a day that earned me seventy-five dollars and that was exactly what my rent was for the month.

Of course, I was selling my stuff that I had always called my hoarded treasures at yard sale prices in order to clear it out of my life a box at a time.

I was welcomed as the 'Book Lady' because I had been there occasionally to rent a table in the front of the Market at a daily rate. Many of the vendors knew me in passing but I had never become a constant in their lives until then.

It felt good to be the 'Book Lady' and to finally have a place to go every Saturday, Sunday, and Monday. Of course, when the weather turned from winter to spring, my Saturday attendance would be sporadic, but I could still be there on Sunday and Monday.

"Hey, Ellen, do you need some help?" asked David as I struggled to pull the loaded shopping cart I had collected from inside the Market so I could load it up through the doorway while holding the door open with my backside.

"Sure, I would love some help. I'll unload this stuff and then I'll be right back," I said as I hurried along to get to my Booth 32.

When my hands were finally empty, I held my arms out to let David know I wanted a hug. I had become a huggy, feely person since my husband's death. I wanted nothing else, just the comfort of being held momentarily by another human being. It was my equivalent of 'hi'.

David, a man of about five-seven in stature with sparkling, happy eyes, was soon to be celebrating his eighty-sixth birthday, so going the next step was out of the question with him. I was truly sorry there was a twenty-two-year difference in our ages. I would have liked to have taken the next step with him. Needless to say, he will forever remain my friend.

The next person to speak to me was Junior, who towered over me at plus or minus six feet to my five-one. He, too, was a huggy, feely person but I believe his motive was different from mine. I could tell from the all-embracing hugs that he was striving for a little more than I was willing to share. Maybe someday, after I get to know him a little better and my feeling of cheating on Sonny goes away, if ever. Then again, maybe not, especially since I had discovered he was married.

Companionship was what I wanted, definitely not a replacement for Sonny. That made me hard to pin down as far as men were concerned because I just wasn't interested in a full time commitment. I definitely was not interested in a married man.

"You are a pretty woman," said Junior as he folded over a bit to give me a hug.

"Thanks, Junior, but I think you might need some new glasses," I said as I pulled myself from his grasp.

CHAPTER 33

MEET THE VENDORS

The women I talked with at the Market were a little more reserved. Eventually, they warmed up a bit to talk with me.

Reba and Larry, her husband, were the persons in charge when the owners, Bob and Judy, weren't present. Both Reba and Larry appeared to be a little stand-offish in that you had to speak to them first and even at that you rarely received more than a one-word response. Once the ice was broken, the conversation flowed freely.

I knew stand-offish because I had been that way most of my life. I was a wallflower. I would stand to the side and watch the world with its many scenarios unfold before me. I would join in, if approached, but most of the time I relished the watching.

I had to force myself to become noticeable, perhaps aggressive, so I could influence the passersby to stop and look at the writings I had to offer. That was hard, at first, but it made me become a relevant part of my world.

My booth was located in the back of the enormous building almost in the center. I was able to see all the way to the front entrance if the rows between me and the front were open meaning the occupants were present and selling their wares with the rolling doors up.

On the same row with me and to my right was Evan, a woodworker who specialized in primitive motif. Like me, he hadn't been in the booth very long and was bringing in new offerings each time he came to sell.

126

To my left was a space that was filled with spillover from another vendor, meaning the space was for rent to anyone seeking space.

The next booth passed the spillover space was occupied by Gail and her selection of jewelry, clothes for children, and other miscellaneous items. Gail was a talker who had an opinion about everyone and everything. I was a listener so I got to hear all of the background of her confrontations with vendors, family, and friends. It made for some really interesting listening.

Across from me to my left was Frances who was an elderly lady that sold just about anything from small hand tools to knick-knacks.

Next to Frances was Brenda who had three spaces containing primitive décor.

Next to Brenda was Peggy, a long-time acquaintance of mine whose son was my son's best friend in their youth.

As long as I let all of those personalities simmer in their own spaces, I felt I could get along with them. After all, they were here first.

I remained in the wallflower mode when I was with the vendors but instantly changed to an outgoing, engaging woman so I could flag down the customers and invite them to look at my writings and stuff, the other items I was selling.

I was secreted in my booth, sitting at the small wooden tray table I had brought from home so I would have a place to write.

Each one of my books was represented by a copy placed on its own individual stand for people to see and pick up for inspection. They were all lined up in two rows on the four-foot table directly in front of my writing table.

Behind me and to each side were items that I call 'stuff', meaning good items that I no longer wanted or needed ranging from compact discs to handbags and all junk in between.

The sales were brisk for my 'stuff' but slow for the books which was what I thought it would be.

I would sit at my writing table and write some more on my book, this one to be truthful, or short stories for contests and sometimes a poem or two.

I wasn't paying attention to my surroundings, which was my mistake. When I finally looked up because I felt a presence, I caught a glimpse of a dark, hoodie-clad figure just disappearing from my sight line.

"Oh my God," I whispered as the image of the dark, hoodie-clad figure finally penetrated my brain.

I stood up so I could get out from behind the two tables and hurried to the doorway to try to catch another glimpse.

The layout of the Market was like a maze. A newcomer could lose his bearings easily but those of us who have been here several times knew our way around to where all of the hiding places were located.

"Gail, could you keep an eye on my booth? I think I saw someone I know. I'm going to try to catch up with him. Okay?" I asked the friendliest lady in the group.

"Sure, go ahead," Gail said with a wave of her hand.

I took off into the direction that I had seen him or her walk.

How in the world did he find me? Why?

CHAPTER 34

THE CHASE IS ON

This was a busy day at the Market. I knew I was losing customers by not being present in my booth but I had to know who was stalking me and why?

I turned my head from side to side as I made a right turn from Booth 32 and walked slowly, glimpsing inside each opened, roll-top doorway to catch another glimpse of my stalker.

There were 92 rentable booths in this building and I was afraid I was going to have to check each and every one of them.

My gut feeling told me he or she, whatever, was still here; still watching me.

Thankfully not all of the spaces were filled with vendors so an empty booth was opened and displayed.

Some of the rolling doors were closed and that meant that someone was probably using the place for temporary storage, at least, until the space was rented to a new arrival.

Then, I would get to the spaces that were full of wares and people browsing through them. They were the hardest ones to check out because my stalker could easily blend in with the removal of the hoodie.

When I reached the end of my booth row, I turned left and walked to the next long row to continue my search.

"Junior, did you see someone walk by here wearing a black hoodie?" I asked as I reached Junior's Booth 67.

"Yeah, I did. He went walking that way," he said as he pointed to the opposite direction from which I had come.

"Did you recognize the person?" I asked in a whisper.

"No, can't say that I did. I don't believe I've ever seen him before," he answered.

"Are you sure it was a man?" I asked as I stopped in front of Junior for an answer.

"I can't rightfully say that for sure. It looked like a man but nowadays women dress like men. You know how that is," he said with a laugh.

"That way?" I asked as I pointed straight ahead.

He shook his head and I walked on swiveling my head back and forth searching each booth I was passing.

I walked a little further and saw Brenda talking to Carlies.

"Brenda, Carlies, did you see a man with a black hoodie walk past you?" I asked as I approached the two of them.

Carlies shook his head from side to side indicating the negative. It was likely that if my stalker were a man, he would not be looking through the contents of Booth 14 from which Carlies sold Avon products.

Brenda motioned that the man I was talking about walked on down the hallway which was almost to the end of the row where I would turn left and continue to the next row. That row would take me to the open space tables in the front that were rented on a daily basis for the occasional vendor who didn't want to be obligated to a three-day event every week.

I didn't see him in the open area so I continued down the other half of the row that was filled with booths, vendors, and customers.

This row was where David's Booth 62 and his buddy, Albert, the bird house builder in Booth 63 next to him, were located.

"What's your hurry?" David asked as I started past his booth.

"Looking for somebody," I whispered.

"Who?" David asked.

"A man wearing a black hoodie. Did you see him?" I asked as I continued to walk slowly.

"Yeah, keep walking. He's not far ahead of you," David told me.

I walked down to the end of the row and turned left to the last half row before I would get to the lobby area and front entrance.

"I'd better find him soon," I mumbled. "I'm almost out of the building."

I walked past the reduced-price drug store items and Beth's Antler Creations reaching the lobby and the people milling around the open space sales area filled with the gun sellers.

It was going to be a challenge trying to spot a dark, hoodie-clad figure among the gun sellers and buyers because they all seemed to fit that description.

I tried to find my way through the milling men. Then I caught a glimpse of a black hoodie.

"Let me through," I shouted at the man in front of me who had stopped to inspect a gun.

"Sure, lady," he said as he stepped aside.

I thought I missed my opportunity. I thought he had had a chance to slip out of the front door.

I strained to my tiptoes and tried to look over the heads of the people moving around in front of me.

"Hey you!" I shouted when I saw the black hoodie.

I saw him move on to walk past the closed snack bar and in front of the upper level booths around part of the shorter outside wall. These were the special booths that were equipped with electricity.

My steps slowed a bit. Did I really want to catch this character that has been a ghostly shadow in my life for months and months?

"Keep going, Ellen," I said as I tried to spur myself to continue on to the final row, the very last one behind my booth. It was a row on which all of the overhead doors were closed, some locked, because no one had ever rented them other than for storage since the Indoor Market opened. It was too far back off of the beaten path away from the customers in search of bargains.

CHAPTER 35

WHY?

"HEY, YOU!" I shouted again through the echoing hallway.

The dark, hoodie-clad figure came to an abrupt halt not fifty feet in front of me with his back to me.

When I looked past him, I saw David and Junior blocking his path.

Then the dark, hoodie-clad figure turned toward me.

I walked closer to get a good look at my stalker.

"Who are you?" I demanded.

The dark, hoodie-clad figure jerked on his hood and pulled it away from his face.

"I'm not sure you remember me," he said apologetically. "I'm John Smith."

My jaw dropped as I recognized him.

"Why have you been stalking me?" I shouted angrily.

"I'm not a stalker," said John Smith. "I'm a fan. I really like your books and I really like you."

"Why have you been hiding in the shadows and covering your head so I couldn't recognize you?" I continued in loud words.

"You didn't want to see me anymore. You didn't want me to talk to you. You really didn't give me any other choice," he said apologetically.

"My God," I said in a quieter tone, "I thought you were trying to do me harm."

David and Junior had moved on after figuring out that I wasn't in danger.

"I wouldn't hurt you, Ellen. I was trying to get up the courage to invite you to dinner," he said softly.

"Really?" I said as my heart began to melt. I remembered how much I had missed his appearance at the book signings and how I had searched for his face many times after I had told him to go away.

"Walk me back to my booth and I'll give you a business card with my phone number on it. Call me," I said as I moved ahead of him.

"That's great," he said. "That way you can get to know me and you'll find out that I meant no harm."

"Is your name really John Smith?" I said when we reached my booth and I handed him my card.

"Yes, it is, believe it or not," he answered.

"I suppose you followed my itinerary from the information I posted on the computer," I said as I continued to probe.

"I sure did," he said. "You certainly are a busy lady."

"That I am, John Smith."

John Smith pulled his wallet from his back pocket and inserted my business card.

"Will you be home this evening?" he asked as he turned to leave.

"Yes sir," I answered.

"I'll call you later," he said and was gone.

When I was getting ready to leave my booth for the day, I looked under my table to see what I had been kicking while I was talking with John Smith.

"I found it," I whispered as I pulled my missing tote containing my binder from beneath the table. I had no idea how or when it was placed under my table or by whom because I could have been the culprit. I easily could have grabbed it up when I was moving my books and stuff to the All Seasons Indoor Market. Right?

I went home with a smile on my face.

I found my missing binder and John Smith had returned.

It was good day.

OTHER BOOKS WRITTEN BY LINDA HUDSON HOAGLAND:

FICTION

ONWARD AND UPWARD

MISSING SAMMY

AN UNJUST COURT

SNOOPING CAN BE DOGGONE DEADLY

SNOOPING CAN BE DEVIOUS

SNOOPING CAN BE CONTAGIOUS

SNOOPING CAN BE DANGEROUS

THE BEST DARN SECRET

CHECKING ON THE HOUSE

DEATH BY COMPUTER

THE BACKWARDS HOUSE

AN AWFULLY LONELY PLACE

Linda Hudson Hoagland

NONFICTION

90 YEARS AND STILL GOING STRONG

QUILTED MEMORIES

LIVING LIFE FOR OTHERS

JUST A COUNTRY BOY: DON DUNFORD (Edited)

WATCH OUT FOR EDDY

THE LITTLE OLD LADY NEXT DOOR

COLLECTIONS

I AM LINDA ELLEN…(POETRY)

A COLLECTION OF WINNERS (SHORT PROSE)

Crooked Road Stalker

Made in the USA
Monee, IL
05 November 2021